THE MOST POWERFUL OF KINGS

JACKIE ASHENDEN

MILLS & BOON

First published in Great Britain 2020
by Mills & Boon, an imprint of HarperCollins*Publishers*
1 London Bridge Street, London, SE1 9GF

Large Print edition 2021

© 2020 Jackie Ashenden

ISBN: 978-0-263-08991-2

MIX
Paper from
responsible sources
FSC **FSC C007454**
www.fsc.org

This book is produced from independently certified FSC™ paper to ensure responsible forest management. For more information visit www.harpercollins.co.uk/green.

Printed and bound in Great Britain
by CPI Group (UK) Ltd, Croydon, CR0 4YY

For the 300

CHAPTER ONE

ANNA FLEETWOOD STOOD by the window in the great medieval fortress that was the royal palace of Axios, staring down at the little city nestled at the foot of the mountains below, the white stone buildings glowing in the sun, the windows glittering.

Itheus. Capital city of Axios, a small, but pretty kingdom just over Greece's northern border.

She would have liked to do a few tourist-type things, since this was her first time out of England and away from the convent she'd grown up in, but unfortunately she wasn't here to play the tourist.

She was here to meet King Adonis Nikolaides, the Lion of Axios.

She took a breath, trying to resist the urge to rub her sweaty palms down her plain grey dress.

Of course she wasn't nervous. He was only a king. No big deal.

Anna turned from the window.

The big room she stood in was the king's receiving room, with walls of undressed stone and a stone floor. Some attempts at lightening the austerity had been made with a few silk rugs, a couple of ancient-looking tapestries depicting battle scenes, and an incongruous spray of orchids on a side table near the huge fireplace.

But even the bright sun pouring through the window couldn't soften the hard, very masculine energy of the room—of the entire palace, truth be told—and she was beginning to see why the Mother Superior of her convent had asked her to come to Axios.

The king needed someone to be a companion for his young daughter and, as the king's godmother, the Reverend Mother had decided to undertake finding someone herself. She'd consequently decided that Anna was perfect for the job, despite Anna's clear lack of anything resembling experience with either teaching or children. Anna had tried to argue, of course, but the Reverend Mother wouldn't listen. And somehow a meeting was arranged, and Anna found herself on a flight to Axios, a thick guidebook—the Reverend Mother eschewed technology—her only reading material.

Anna wandered over to one of the tapestries and examined it. It was very old, depicting a gory battle scene with people getting their heads lopped off with broad swords, and arrows embedding themselves in heads through visors of helmets.

She wondered which particular battle this one depicted, since the history of Axios seemed to be nothing but non-stop wars and skirmishes. An austere, military culture, according to the guidebook. Just like its king, by all accounts.

Anna squinted at the figure standing in the middle of the battle scene: a giant warrior wearing one of those ancient Greek horsehair helmets, his huge arms raised above his head, a massive sword held between them. Another warrior lay at his feet, hands lifted, either trying to stop an attack or beg for mercy, it wasn't clear.

What was clear was that there would be no mercy coming from the giant warrior.

A shiver of foreboding snaked down Anna's

spine, which she ignored. How silly. It was just a tapestry.

She leaned forward for a closer examination—and maybe to prove to herself that the shiver had been an aberration—then wrinkled her nose. It was musty.

'Something about our history you don't approve of?' a voice said from behind her, deep and harsh, like a glacier scraping over stone.

Anna's heart leapt into her mouth and she froze, a primitive, animal part of her sensing threat. Had she done something wrong? Was she not supposed to be here? Had she touched something she shouldn't have? She hadn't heard anyone come in…

There was silence behind her.

She took a breath, her heart thumping, and turned around.

A bolt of pure, instinctive fear shot through her, because somehow the huge warrior on the tapestry had come to life and was standing a few feet away from her by the door.

He was a giant of a man, standing at over six feet four at least, with the kind of wide, heavily muscled shoulders and broad chest that she'd always imagined Atlas possessing, strong enough to carry the entire world on his back. His waist was narrow, his legs long and solid and powerful; he looked as if he could complete two marathons in a row without even breaking a sweat.

His features were roughly carved with a brutal, masculine kind of handsomeness: strong jaw, a blade of a nose, closely cropped black hair, straight dark brows, deep-set, piercing eyes the blue of a cold winter sky. And he radiated authority and power the way the sun radiated heat. It was almost a physical force, making her want to go to her knees and pray before him as she did before the altar in church.

The king.

Of course it was the king. She'd read up on him in the guidebook and it had to be said that the pictures of him, grim-faced and utterly impassive, looking as if he hadn't ever smiled one day in his life, didn't do him justice. They didn't capture that aura of power.

He looked as if he'd been born wearing a crown.

Her mouth had dried and her palms had got even sweatier, and she was a little appalled at herself and her ridiculous burst of fear. Because, though he might look as if he was more suited to the battlefield on the tapestry behind her than he was to a throne room, he wasn't going to do anything to her.

She bobbed a graceless curtsey. 'Um, sorry, Your Majesty. I was just admiring the...um... tapestry.'

He said nothing, his granite features utterly expressionless, his blue eyes glacial. He wore a conventional yet immaculately tailored suit of charcoal-grey wool, black business shirt and a tie of dull gold silk.

How strange. She'd been positive it was armour he'd been wearing when she'd first looked at him.

Don't get carried away.

No, of course not. She was flighty and prone to an overactive imagination, as the Reverend Mother had always said in kind yet slightly disappointed tones, and she needed to work on controlling her impulses and passions, since those only led to trouble.

Then again, it had been years since she'd been that young, wild girl who used to sing too loudly in the choir, talk too much at mealtimes, accidentally knock over the communion wine, and get grass stains on her habit.

She'd made a decision a year ago that it was a life of contemplation and prayer that she wanted, and had asked the Reverend Mother to approve her taking her vows.

The Reverend Mother had had other plans for her, however, such as a visit to Axios and 'some time away in the secular world', before making her final decision.

Anna had been frustrated because she didn't need 'time in the secular world' but, since she couldn't take her vows without the Reverend Mother's approval, she'd had no choice but to do what she was told.

Which meant comporting herself as befitted a nun rather than an untried novice.

'Anna Fleetwood, I presume?' the king said.

Anna inclined her head. 'Yes, Your Majesty.'

He eyed her dispassionately for a second then raised a hand, indicating one of the armchairs near the couch. 'Please, sit.'

She supposed the 'please' was for form's sake, since it didn't sound like a request. More like an order.

She'd never been particularly obedient—something else that concerned the Reverend Mother—but she went without even her usual irritation at being told what to do, moving over to the armchair the king had indicated.

It was a heavy piece of furniture, covered in dark leather and not particularly comfortable. Anna perched on the edge of the seat, clasping her hands together in her lap, watching as the king went to the couch and sat down. For all his height and muscular size, he moved with a kind of lethal, animal grace that she found oddly mesmerising.

The Lion of Axios, that was what they called him, and that was what he reminded her of: a great, predatory beast.

Which makes you a gazelle.

Anna didn't much like that comparison. She didn't want to get eaten and she didn't want to be hunted. What she wanted was to do the job the Reverend Mother had assigned her and then return to England to take her vows. Easy.

'So, Sister,' the king said in his deep, harsh voice, his English perfect and uninflected. 'I assume the Reverend Mother told you what is required for the position you'll be taking?'

Actually, the Reverend Mother had been frustratingly opaque about it, merely assuring Anna that she would be perfect for the position no

matter her inexperience and that the king—
or more probably one of his staff members—
would give her all the details.

But, on arrival at the palace, no one had given
her any details. She had simply been ushered
straight into the receiving room to wait for the
king without a word.

Nervousness fluttered in her gut.

She hadn't much experience with men, still
less with men who looked like him, and none
at all when it came to royalty. And he was so
very royal and so very…male.

He made her uncomfortable.

'A little,' Anna said, forcing the feeling away.
'The Reverend Mother mentioned teaching the
princess.' And then, because she was incurably
honest and wanted him to know, she added, 'I
should warn you, Your Majesty, that I don't
have any teaching experience. Or any experience with children at all, in fact.'

The king said nothing, merely looked at her,
and Anna tried to stop herself fidgeting under
the weight of that icy blue gaze.

'The position doesn't involve teaching,' he
said after a long moment. 'The princess al-

ready has a tutor. I require a more…steadying influence.'

Anna frowned. 'Excuse me, Your Majesty? I'm not quite sure—'

He lifted a hand. 'You may address me as sire if it's easier.'

'Very well, sire,' she said. 'And, please, call me Anna.' She didn't much care for being called Sister quite yet, not when she hadn't taken her vows.

'Noted.' He leaned back on the couch, the slight movement making her aware of his long, powerful body, a very physical awareness she'd never experienced with another person before. 'You weren't quite sure of what?'

'What you meant by a "steadying influence".'

'Ah.' He shifted again, very slightly, and again her attention was drawn to the pull of fabric across his broad shoulders and powerful thighs.

Which was strange. Why on earth was she staring at his body? She might not have had much to do with men, it was true, but it wasn't as if she hadn't seen a man before.

Not a man like this one, you haven't.

'Ione's behaviour is an issue,' the king said

without preamble. 'She is a loud, boisterous child, which is not becoming in the heir to the throne. I believe she needs to start learning how to manage herself and her emotions, and, since I do not have the time for it, help is required from an outside source.'

Anna ignored her own odd reaction to him and frowned. Surely, all children were boisterous? Then again, who was she to question a king's parenting decisions?

'I see. And is there anything in particular you'd like me to do?'

'You will be issued with a list of acceptable activities, as well as some rules concerning Ione, her behaviour, and what is permitted and what is not. You will also be assigned a room here in the palace for your personal use.'

Well, that didn't sound…onerous.

Anna opened her mouth to tell him it sounded fine, but before she could he said, 'The Reverend Mother heard that I was looking for a companion for my daughter and chose you specifically for this task.' He paused, his gaze raking over her in a way that made Anna distinctly uncomfortable for reasons she couldn't put her finger on. 'Any idea as to why that might be?'

She felt her cheeks heat. 'No.'

One of the king's black brows arrowed sky-ward. 'No? No idea at all?'

'I... No. I'm not sure.' Her poise, already shaky, began to slip. Because she really had no idea at all why the Reverend Mother had chosen her. She'd been called into her study and given the task, and the Reverend Mother hadn't explained. And Anna hadn't questioned it, too busy trying to prove her obedience.

She had nothing to be ashamed of, so why was she blushing?

'No,' she said more levelly and with greater confidence. 'She didn't tell me and I didn't ask. It wasn't my place. I do as she tells me.'

'I see.' The king's voice was very deep and glazed with ice. 'So nothing at all to do with seducing me into making you my queen?'

The nun's pretty grey eyes went very, very wide.

'I beg your pardon?' she exclaimed, in tones of complete astonishment.

Adonis wasn't a man who repeated himself and he didn't now. He simply stared at her, scanning and assessing her threat level the way he did with everyone he met.

Except the nun—or novice really—didn't pose much of a threat. She wore a plain and unflattering grey dress, her long, pale gold hair coiled in a loose bun at her nape, and she was round and very soft-looking. Her face was pretty, heart-shaped, with a firm chin and those wide eyes the colour of morning fog. Her mouth was a problem, though, full and red and…biteable.

Not that he would be doing any biting. She was a rabbit who'd wandered into a wolf's den, or perhaps even a quail. Soft and round and far too innocent.

Luckily for her this particular wolf wasn't hungry and hadn't been for years, and even if he had been, he wouldn't have chosen such easy prey.

It was very clear that she had no idea what her interfering Reverend Mother had done. But he did. The Reverend Mother June was his god-mother and had been sending him letters ever since his wife had died five years earlier. She'd said they were to 'comfort him in his time of need'. But Adonis didn't need comforting and he didn't need his godmother recommending various women to him as prospects for his next queen. He got far too much of that from his own royal council and their insistence that he take a wife; he didn't need it from one elderly English nun.

Unfortunately, it seemed as if said nun had ignored his gentle but firm commands to mind her own business and had sent him this pretty woman instead.

It was irritating and he was tempted to send her straight back to where she had come from, but if he didn't even grant her an audience, the Reverend Mother would no doubt only send him another sacrificial lamb and he really didn't want an endless procession of novices turning up at his front door.

And there *was* the issue of his daughter, who did, in fact, need a civilising influence.

He opened his mouth to ask her another question about her supposed purpose here when the doors suddenly burst open and a hellion in a blue dress with a plastic breastplate worn over the top, a helmet pressed down over her red curls, and waving a plastic sword came tumbling in.

She screeched to a halt beside the couch, waved the sword threateningly and shouted in Axian, 'Don't move or I'll cut your heads off. Right now!'

The nun's mouth dropped open as she stared at Princess Ione, Lioness of Axios and first in line to the throne.

'Ione,' Adonis growled. 'English, please. And where are your manners?'

His daughter whirled, took in his face, and the sword drooped. 'Sorry, Papa,' she said, switching languages effortlessly and looking contrite. Then she threw her weapon down, came over to the couch, and without even asking climbed into his lap and held a finger up in front of his face. 'My finger hurts. Can you kiss it better?'

She had begun to do this more and more whenever she was in his presence. Reach for his hand. Throw her arms around him. Beg to be picked up. Cry when he told her no and then shout that she hated him, not caring who might be around to note her behaviour.

It was unacceptable. A king was always under threat from enemies and anyone close to him could be a target to be used against him. So he tried to make sure that no one got too close. That had been relatively simple to achieve; he had no close friends anyway and no confidants. No one he trusted. He even kept his younger brother, Prince Xerxes, at arm's length.

Unfortunately, his daughter was too young to understand why this was necessary and why *her* father wasn't the same as other people's, and as she'd grown older she had become needier, and more demanding of him. She wouldn't do what she was told, was wilfully disobedient, had screaming tantrums loud enough to wake the dead, and he'd been forced to come to the conclusion that she needed taking in hand.

He'd hoped not to use the methods his own father had used on him, since they were a blunt instrument at best, and Ione was still too young for that anyway. He'd opted for a...gentler way. A meek, obedient nun, for example.

Whatever the case, Ione needed to learn control, how to detach herself from her emotions, because a monarch could not be ruled by their heart.

He had learned. So could she.

He ignored her finger just as he ignored the

urge to kiss it better. Those fatherly impulses were strong, but he was stronger.

'You cannot sit on me, Ione,' Adonis said, gently putting his daughter back on her feet again. 'How many times must I tell you?'

Ione's jaw got that pugnacious look, which usually heralded a tantrum, so he distracted her. 'This lady is Sister Anna. She might be here to be your friend.'

The tactic worked. Ione forgot her finger and looked over at the little nun. 'Her? But she doesn't even have a sword,' she said, somewhat disdainfully.

At that point, the nun seemed to break out of her paralysis and smiled.

And Adonis felt something inside him flicker, like a spark in a cold, dead hearth.

Because that smile was breathtaking. It lit up her face, turning it from pretty to stunning in seconds flat, those fog-grey eyes glittering with silver fire.

It felt as if the sun had come into the room.

'Hello,' the nun said to his daughter. 'You can call me Anna, if you like. What's your name?'

'Princess Ione,' Ione answered regally.

'What a pretty name. I heard you were a lioness.' The nun leaned forward slightly. 'Can you roar?'

'Yes!' Ione said, suddenly animated. 'Would you like to hear it?'

'Oh, yes, please.'

Ione roared obligingly and very, very loudly.

The nun clapped her hands and looked delighted. 'What a magnificent roar.'

'Ione,' Adonis said firmly, deciding to cut short this particular meeting. 'Please go and find Hesta. Miss Angela will be waiting for you in the schoolroom.'

Hesta was one of Ione's guards and probably responsible for his daughter's sudden interest in weapons. Adonis was not opposed to it, but Ione was still struggling with reading and that, surely, was more important.

'But—' Ione began.

'Now,' Adonis said.

His daughter made a grumpy sound and went disconsolately out through the door.

The nun was still smiling that radiant smile and he had the strangest urge to lift his hands to it, as if it were a fire he could warm himself in front of.

'She's delightful,' the nun said.

'She's a terror,' he disagreed.

Her smile became warmer, the sun shining directly on him. 'I know you wanted to kiss her finger. I hope you didn't stop for my benefit.'

And the spark in the cold, dead hearth of his heart glowed again. He crushed it. No fires could be lit in that fireplace. The only passion a king was permitted was for his country. It was something his father had often said and Adonis agreed.

'You didn't answer my question,' he said expressionlessly.

Sister Anna's lovely smile faltered, and the sun dimmed, as though it went behind a cloud. 'Which particular question?'

'I think you know what I'm talking about.' It was perhaps foolish to push for an answer when it was obvious that she had no idea about the Reverend Mother's real agenda.

Still. He wanted to hear the answer.

She looked away, smoothing her grey dress with her hands. 'The Reverend Mother said nothing to me about…well, you know. She only said something about a tutor for the princess and that I would be a good fit for the position.'

A flush stained her cheekbones, her fingers fussing with the hem of her dress.

It seemed she was uncomfortable with the turn of the conversation, which perversely only made him want to continue it. He couldn't fathom why. He had a great many other things to do that were much more important than making a pretty nun blush.

'I see.' He should end this conversation and dismiss her, yet he didn't. 'So nothing at all about the best way to seduce me, then?'

She flushed an even deeper shade of pink, her fingers furiously pleating the hem of her skirt.

It was wrong of him to tease a woman this innocent. That was more his brother's mode of behaviour—though, now Xerxes had married, he didn't do that so much any more. But the prince was more handsome and possessed far more charm than Adonis ever had. He was... fun. Adonis had never seen the point of fun.

Annoyed with himself, he was about to end the conversation, when suddenly the little nun met his gaze, her eyes full of what looked like temper. 'No, Your Majesty,' she said flatly. 'The Reverend Mother said nothing about seduction and it would be highly improper of her to do so even if she had.' She gave him a severe look. 'Why on earth would you think that's what I'm here for?'

Adonis stared at her in surprise. He was the king. Everyone was afraid of him and he didn't mind that. His entire purpose was to protect his country and put its interests first. He didn't need to be loved or even liked; what he needed was to be obeyed, and if respect didn't make that happen, then he'd settle for fear. He wasn't fussy.

But right now there was neither respect nor fear in the little nun's disconcertingly direct gaze, only offended dignity and outrage.

Another man might have apologised. But kings never apologised and neither did Adonis. In fact, far from prompting shame, the expression on her face instead ignited a small, electric jolt of sensation centred in much lower, baser parts of his body.

'Then what are you here for?' he asked, before he could stop himself.

The little nun drew herself up in her chair, lifting that determined and very firm chin. 'I'm here to help you with the princess,' she said with dignity. 'Just like the Reverend Mother ordered me to.'

'And do you do everything you're ordered to do?'

'Of course.' Her hands rearranged themselves in her lap. 'I shall be taking my vows soon and proving my obedience is one of the tasks I need to undertake before the Reverend Mother gives her approval.'

You could show her how to be obedient.

The thought was instinctive and so unexpected he sat there for a minute in shock at his own response.

He was a man who was in complete control of himself and his environment. A man who didn't suffer from sparks in the dead area of his chest where his heart should be. Or flickers of sexual interest in small, innocent creatures such as the one sitting opposite him. He had his hungers, but they were entirely physical and when his body needed a release he dealt with it either himself, or with a couple of very discreet, experienced women who were happy to see him when he needed them, and just as happy to say goodbye when he left.

So he didn't know why this particular woman,

this very innocent *nun,* was making him feel things he did not want to feel. In fact, why she should make him feel anything at all was beyond him.

Detachment was the key to being an effective protector and defender of his country, and so he didn't let anything touch him. His father, King Xenophon, had been a hard and brutal teacher on that specific point, but Adonis had learned. He might once have raged against his father's methods, yet in the end he'd come to see the importance of it.

He felt nothing. And one little novice nun wasn't going to change that.

Ignoring the flickers of interest from his baser self, Adonis said curtly, 'Then you can prove yourself obedient by obeying my order to leave Axios.'

This time it was her turn to stare at him in surprise. 'Excuse me, Your Majesty? Did you—'

'Are you deaf?' he interrupted, suddenly irritated almost into anger at himself and this whole ridiculous situation. 'You will leave Axios by tomorrow morning. Am I clear?'

Shock rippled over her face, swiftly followed by another deep flush.

'I'm sorry if I caused offence, sire.' The spark of anger had vanished from her voice, leaving nothing but contrition. 'I spoke out of turn.'

She was absolutely genuine, of that there was no doubt. And if he'd been a man who felt normal human emotion, he might have felt sorry for her.

But he wasn't and he didn't.

Instead, he pushed himself to his feet. 'Tomorrow morning,' he said flatly.

Then he turned on his heel and left the room.

CHAPTER TWO

ANNA PACED AROUND the little guest room she'd been shown to after her failed audience with the king, anger churning in her gut.

She hated him. He was cold, rude, arrogant, autocratic. And, even though he might have looked as if he was going to kiss his adorable little daughter's finger, he hadn't. Certainly, he had no business accusing her of being here only to seduce him. What absolute rot. She was a novice nun, not a pretty socialite or member of the aristocracy trying for a good marriage.

She wanted to take her vows, not...seduce men.

It was absurd that he'd even considered it. Though now she was curious as to why he'd even think that in the first place. Perhaps the Reverend Mother had sent other novices to him. She hadn't heard of any, though, and anyway, why would the Reverend Mother send her if that was the case?

Sister Caroline was much lovelier than she was and Sister Maria was more refined. There was nothing about Anna to recommend her to a king.

She came to a stop near the door and glared at it.

Now she was to be sent home for absolutely no reason that she could see. Why? Did he not believe her when she said she'd obeyed the Reverend Mother? Or had he been offended by her outburst?

A trickle of shame slid slowly down her back.

She shouldn't have let her annoyance at him get the better of her, especially given it was his daughter's behaviour that he wanted her help with. Not exactly the best example to set. She'd only been shocked by his accusation and offended, if the truth be told. She wasn't a seductress in any way, shape or form.

And you definitely did not think about what it might be like to seduce him...

Anna whirled away from the door, going over to the heavy wooden bed. Her battered suitcase sat on the thick white linen quilt and she flung it open, digging pointlessly around inside it.

No, she hadn't thought about seducing him.

She was a novice wanting to take her vows and she'd eschewed earthly pleasures. Not that she had any experience with said earthly pleasures, and not that she'd ever wanted to.

She knew about sex from a biological point of view and had sneaked a few romances from some of the other novices, so she'd learned about passion too. But that hadn't been enough to make her think she wanted a man in her life.

The Reverend Mother had mentioned following a vocation and Anna had decided that her vocation lay in the convent.

She'd grown up with the sisters, having been taken in as a baby after her mother had given birth to her before promptly disappearing. A year earlier Anna had tracked her down, wanting to find out her own history, and initially her mother had been receptive to the emails Anna had sent. Then, inexplicably, had cut off all contact, mentioning another family and a life she didn't want disrupted.

Not so inexplicably.

Perhaps if Anna hadn't indulged her temper and been impatient when her mother had mentioned old memories being stirred up, that contact wouldn't have been cut off.

But it was too late now. She'd got angry and her mother hadn't contacted her again, and now Anna had added forgiveness to the list of virtues she needed to practise.

It was fine. Her mother had found the contact too difficult, and she was totally within her rights not to want to continue it. Anna didn't need her acceptance to find a home, anyway. She'd found her place with the sisters and that was where she was going to stay.

And she definitely wasn't going to be leaving that for a mere man.

No matter how interesting the man?

Anna shut her case firmly. There were no interesting men. And that included the arrogant, rude king with the ridiculous Christian name.

It felt grossly unfair that he was going to send her away without a reason. What would she tell the Reverend Mother? It had been her rudeness that had caused her dismissal in all likelihood, which wouldn't go down at all well. Especially when everyone knew what a temper she had.

Perhaps the Reverend Mother would even decide not to approve Anna taking her vows, which would be…

A cold feeling twisted in her gut. She would

be cast out into the world to find her own way, with no friends and no family. Locked out of the only home she'd ever known.

She couldn't let that happen, she just couldn't. Which meant she'd have to go to this king and ask him for a reason for her dismissal. She deserved that much, didn't she? After coming all the way here? And if she knew the reason, then perhaps she could convince him to let her stay.

Anna stalked over to the door and pulled it open, glancing down the stone corridor. The palace was medieval, with high, vaulted ceilings and narrow stone hallways. There were lights, but it was a place that brought to mind flickering sconces and rushes on the floor, with lots of hounds and burly men in armour milling around.

She walked quickly, confident she'd find someone who'd point her in the right direction. Palaces were generally full of people, after all. They'd no doubt forbid her to see the king, since she supposed a nobody like her wouldn't be granted a second audience. Nevertheless, she was prepared to stand her ground. Even five minutes of his time for an explanation would be enough.

A few palace staff were around, but none of them were forthcoming about where the king was—understandably—but after she'd smiled winningly at one stern-faced guard he mentioned that the king was having some 'sparring' time in the gym.

Anna thanked him and went off down another corridor, pausing to ask another guard where the gym was. It was in a different wing of the palace, involving more corridors and a lot of stairs, and when she got to the doors she was stymied by a couple of guards who scanned her suspiciously.

However, she must have looked unthreatening, because after she gave them both another of those winning smiles and played the nun card one of them agreed to take her into the gym to request a personal audience.

The gym turned out to be a huge stone hall, with state-of-the-art exercise machines and weight benches down one end and a big open space covered by a mat near by. Right in front of her, though, was a boxing ring.

Several people stood around it, leaning on the ropes and watching the two men in the middle of the ring. One was a powerful-looking guard.

The other was the king.

Back in the receiving room, he'd been a still presence, projecting a cold, dominant authority. And apart from that one instant when she thought he might have kissed Ione's finger, there had been no warmth to him. Almost nothing human. As if he was a god to be worshipped, not a man to relate to.

But not here.

Now that he was stripped to the waist, wearing black and gold boxing shorts, boxing gloves on his hands, and circling his opponent, that cold authority was gone. There was nothing but the lethal intent and aggression of a large and very hungry predator.

His olive skin glistened, outlining every single hard, carved muscle of his arms and torso; he looked as if he'd been chiselled out of solid rock. He moved so fluidly, all deadly athletic grace that was mesmerising to watch, and, as he circled around, Anna noticed that he had a tattoo inked across the top of his powerful back: a crowned and prowling lion.

Someone made a soft sound and it couldn't have been her, absolutely not.

She abhorred violence.

Yet she couldn't take her eyes off the king.

Heat rushed into her face and she knew she'd gone scarlet, but she still couldn't look away. The lights of the gym glistened on his skin, and she followed every flex and release of those powerful muscles.

She'd never thought of a man being beautiful before, and when she'd first seen him in the receiving room all she'd been conscious of was his authority and power. But she was thinking it now.

Here, like this, all deadly grace and honed aggression, he was beautiful.

She started towards him, barely conscious of moving, but then the guard beside her said gruffly, 'Stay here, Sister. I'll speak to His Majesty.'

So she paused, her heart thumping as the guard approached the boxing ring. One of the men standing by the ropes held up a hand and the guard stopped.

For a second no one moved, and Anna discovered she was holding her breath.

Then the king abruptly burst into motion: a pivot, a turn, ducking under his opponent's guard, drawing his right fist back and slamming it hard into the other man's jaw. The man dropped like a stone.

Everyone watching cheered while the king went down on one knee beside his opponent's recumbent body and issued a sharp order. One of the watching men jumped into the ring, checking over the stunned man, who finally groaned. The king offered him a hand and pulled him to his feet. The king said something and the man grinned.

Anna's heartbeat was so loud she was certain the entire gym could hear it, and there was a fluttery feeling in her stomach, something like nervousness yet not. It was more similar to excitement, though that was strange, because why would she get excited about a boxing match?

The guard approached the ring and the king put his gloved hands on the ropes, leaning down as the guard said something to him. Then his head came up and he looked straight at Anna.

Electric-blue eyes pierced her right through.

She couldn't breathe. All the air had somehow vanished from her lungs, from the entire room, the sound of her heartbeat the only thing she could hear.

The king straightened, still staring at her.

'Out,' he said. And instantly everyone headed towards the doors.

Anna made as if to go too, in instinctive obedience.

'Not you, Sister,' the king said.

Anna froze.

'Come here,' he ordered as the last person left the gym.

She didn't want to. Something instinctive and very female told her that getting close to him would be a bad idea. But she couldn't disobey a king's command and, since she was the one who'd requested this meeting, she forced herself to move, walking slowly over the stone floor to the ring.

He leaned on the ropes, the lines of abs, biceps and sinews flexing, watching her every step of the way, making her feel like a mouse creeping closer to a huge, hungry cat.

She resented it. Being meek was yet another lesson the Reverend Mother wanted her to learn, a lesson Anna had always struggled with. Yet she tried to think of that lesson now as she went over to the king, her head bowed, resisting the urge to meet his gaze in instinctive rebellion.

He said nothing as she reached the ropes, and she suspected that silence might be a deliberate tactic of his to make people feel uncomfortable.

If so, it certainly wasn't going to work with her.

Despite her best intentions, Anna raised her head, meeting that intense blue gaze.

The force of his will almost flattened her.

'Was I not clear?' the king said finally, in his deep, harsh voice. 'Do you want me to tell you again that I wish you to return to England? I hope not. I'm not accustomed to repeating myself.'

Annoyance arrowed down her spine, and before she could stop herself she'd snapped, 'And I'm not accustomed to being sent away without an explanation like a naughty child.'

A crashing silence fell.

Anna's cheeks, already hot, felt as if they were going to burst into flames.

You idiot. He's the king. You can't snap at him like that.

Slowly, he pushed himself away from the ropes, straightening to his full, impressive height, making her feel very, very small.

'Come here,' he ordered.

Obviously he meant, come into the ring.

Briefly, Anna entertained a fantasy of ignoring him, turning her back and walking out. But that wouldn't get her the explanation she wanted and it certainly wouldn't endear her to the Reverend Mother, so she shoved the fantasy away, found the steps that led to the ring, and tried to get over the ropes in a dignified way. Naturally she failed, ending up clambering awkwardly between them while the king watched her, his arms crossed over his muscled chest.

She was blushing furiously and feeling like an idiot by the time she approached him, both of which made her temper crackle and spit like oil poured into a hot frying pan.

Not good, Anna. Not good.

She had to get herself under control. Especially if she wanted an explanation as to why he was dismissing her, and most especially if she wanted him to change his mind. Because if he needed someone to improve his daughter's behaviour, he was hardly likely to choose a woman who couldn't even manage her own.

She had to set an example.

So she tried to swallow the hot words on her

tongue, and tried to project obedience, meekness, and humility as she gave him a curtsey. 'Your Majesty.'

The king's brutal features betrayed nothing. Instead he held out one gloved hand imperiously, palm up. 'Undo the tie, if you please.'

She blinked, realising that he meant the tie of his boxing glove and that of course he couldn't do it himself. But it wasn't until she took a step forward to untie it for him that she understood her mistake.

He was very close, his magnificently muscled and very bare chest inches away. His olive skin was sheened with perspiration and he smelled of clean male sweat and something sharp and fresh like the sea. It was a very masculine scent and she didn't know why she liked it, but she did.

Her hands shook as she pulled at the tie, the heat coming off him so at odds with the cold air of authority he projected. It disturbed her on some deep level, making her very aware of his height and his power, and how much smaller she was, how vulnerable.

She didn't like it, and yet part of her did. Very much. Which didn't make any sense. What was wrong with her? Why did she suddenly feel like this?

'You have a temper, Sister,' the king said.

Anna, bent over his glove, kept her attention on what she was doing, trying determinedly to ignore his physical presence and its effect on her heartbeat.

You're attracted to him. Not a mystery.

But that was ridiculous. She'd never been attracted to any other man before, so why this one? It was a very bad idea. Especially given who this particular man was.

'I...apologise, Your Majesty,' she said, not feeling particularly apologetic as she tugged on the tie, which appeared to be knotted. 'I spoke out of turn.'

'Yes.' His voice was a deep, vibrating rumble she almost felt in her chest. 'You did. The Reverend Mother chose poorly in sending you. How can you manage my daughter when you cannot even manage yourself?'

It was exactly what she'd been thinking herself, the censure in his tone making her feel as if she were twelve again, hauled into the Reverend Mother's office for yet another transgression, the weight of guilt falling on her at the look of gentle disappointment on the Reverend Mother's face. *'Why can't you be good, Anna? I know you have it in you.'* And her wondering if she really did have it in her, thinking that maybe she was just born bad...

Anger churned inside her at the memories. Anger at herself and her own behaviour, as well as her lack of control over it. She was supposed to be better. She *had* to be better.

'I'm sorry,' she repeated, tugging harder on the glove, the tie finally coming loose. 'It won't happen again.'

'That's twice now, in the space of a few hours.'

Anna pulled at the ties holding the glove closed with slightly more force than necessary, not trusting herself to speak, because he wasn't wrong. She *had* snapped at him twice. Him. A king.

'I said I was sorry, sire.' She tried to put every ounce of effort she could into sounding as if she meant it, but she had a suspicion that it only sounded sulky.

'Are you?' He lifted the glove and jerked it off his hand with his teeth, discarding it on the floor of the ring. 'You don't look very sorry to me.'

That flutter deep inside her sparked to life again and she couldn't for the life of her imagine why. Because he was standing there, huge and muscular, intensely masculine, power in every line of him, a very clear and physical threat. And she should be afraid of him, or at least intimidated, yet she wasn't.

Deciding that honesty was the best policy and, since she couldn't pretend, she said, 'You're right. I'm not sorry. I'm angry. I don't like being accused of seducing men I've never even met before.' She lifted her chin. 'Need I remind you that I am a novice, who'll be taking her vows imminently?'

Something glittered in the ice of his blue eyes.

'Not quite as biddable as you would appear, are you?' His intent stare made the fire in her cheeks burn hot. 'Is that why you forced your way in here? To chastise me?'

'I didn't force my way in and no, I'm not here to ch-chastise you.' She wasn't sure why she stumbled over the word, yet charged on anyway. 'I only wanted a reason for you sending me away. The Reverend Mother will be very upset with me if I come back only a day or two after being sent here, and she'll want to know why.'

He lifted one powerful shoulder and glanced away, pulling on the tie of his other glove. 'That's not my problem.'

Anna was suddenly very tempted to kick this irritating king in the shins. 'Actually, sire, it's very much your problem. Especially since I came here in good faith.'

This time the ice in his eyes had melted, blue sparks flicking in the depths. 'Then perhaps you should talk to my dear godmother about meddling in affairs that don't concern her.'

'What affairs?'

'She wants me to remarry.' He bared his teeth in what looked like a smile but was far too feral to be one. 'And, since I have rebuffed her every suggestion, she's now taking the direct approach. With you.'

Anna blinked, the words not making any sense. 'Me?'

'Yes, you.' The king tore the other glove off and cast it on the floor, flexing one strong, long-fingered hand. 'You're round and soft and sweet. Just the kind of woman who would appeal to me.'

She stared, conscious that she was gaping at him yet unable to stop herself.

His gaze became electric. 'Perhaps you should try some seduction, little nun. We wouldn't want to upset the Reverend Mother, now, would we?'

Adonis knew he shouldn't have said it, but the adrenaline high from the workout he'd just had was still coursing through him, and there was something about Sister Anna Fleetwood that got under his skin, that made those flickers of interest he'd felt earlier flare into sparks.

Sparks that could become flames if you're not careful.

But he was always careful. Yet there she was, after elbowing her way into his private workout space, looking up at him all shocked, her cheeks flushed, her gaze gone silvery as it dropped to his chest then back up to his face again, telegraphing loud and clear that she was not as nun-like as she made out.

Innocent, yes.

Immune to him, no.

It was a dangerous thing for him to notice, especially after one of his regular workouts, where he burned off excess anger and aggression in the boxing ring. And most especially when the adrenaline rush made him more susceptible than he'd normally be to physical chemistry.

Which meant he shouldn't be goading her.

Another, more experienced, woman would understand what was going on, but it was plain the nun did not.

'Wh-what do you mean?' she stammered, making that even more obvious.

What are you doing? Since when do you let innocents like this one get to you?

He never did. Sophia, his late, long-suffering wife, hadn't been an innocent and he'd thought she'd known exactly what she was getting into when she married him. He'd told her from the outset that their marriage would be one of necessity only, that love would not be part of it, and she'd assured him that, as she didn't love him, she didn't need it. But then she *had* fallen in love with him, and had been unhappy and hurt when she hadn't got love in return. He didn't want to put another woman through that. He had his heir already, and, now that his brother was married and producing children of his own, Adonis didn't need another wife.

A lover was a different matter, but he wouldn't choose someone like Anna Fleetwood to be his lover anyway. She was too young, too innocent, too soft. She was also a novice nun and under the protection of his godmother, which made her untouchable.

'Never mind,' he said curtly, turning away and stalking over to where his trainer had left a towel hanging over the ropes. He picked it up and used it to wipe his face, before draping it over the back of his neck. 'I don't care what you tell the Reverend Mother when you get back to England. Tell her anything you like.' He paused and turned around to face her. 'But you will be going.'

He couldn't have her here, not when it was plain she was going to be completely unsuitable for Ione anyway. He'd been hoping for meek, biddable, and self-contained, a good example for his daughter to follow, not argumentative, rebellious, and emotionally volatile.

Plus, he didn't want the Reverend Mother thinking she could keep sending him women on the off-chance he'd want to make one of them his wife. He'd already told her he wasn't going to marry again, so why she thought she could change his mind, he had no idea.

The nun frowned, her arms crossed over what he couldn't help but notice were full, generous breasts. Her cheeks were still bright red and her gaze kept dropping to his chest. It made her frown even more ferocious.

'I assure you, Your Majesty, that you are in no danger of being s-seduced by me,' she said very firmly. 'I have no interest in that…kind of thing.'

The way she was staring at him would seem to indicate otherwise, but he couldn't afford to be thinking about that either. What he should be thinking about was perhaps sending a message to Susannah, an American woman he sometimes spent time with, and working out any physical urges with her. She didn't require anything but sex, at least.

'Glad to hear it,' he growled. 'But I'm not changing my mind.'

'What about your daughter?' she shot back, undeterred. 'Who will help you with her? It's clear you do need someone.'

'And you think you're the best person to curtail my daughter's behaviour?' He raised an eyebrow. 'After your own ill-considered outbursts?

She flushed. 'I know it may not seem like it, but I can manage myself. Or is there something else about me that offends you?'

Sneaky little nun. Not only had she lost any respect she might have had for his position, but she was also poking at him in a way she definitely shouldn't. A way that might prompt him to tell her explicitly what offended him about her. Or perhaps even show her...

No. Control yourself.

He gripped the ends of the towel in his hands, forcing down the burn of adrenaline. 'Are you sure you want me to do that? You might not like what I have to say.'

She gave him a challenging look. 'Give me two weeks, Your Majesty. Two weeks to prove that I'm the best person for the job. And if your daughter's behaviour hasn't improved I'll leave, just like you told me to.'

His instinct was to refuse, because once he gave an order he never rescinded it. Then again, his daughter needed someone, and urgently. And insisting on Anna's leaving would be tantamount to admitting that she had got to him, and he couldn't do that either.

She was one little nun. How could a nun—a novice nun at that—have any effect on the years of detachment he'd perfected? She couldn't, so why not let her stay for two weeks? It wasn't long. Enough time to test whether or not she had what it took to manage Ione and her demanding behaviour.

Sister Anna certainly had a few issues with authority that he didn't approve of, then again she was here already, and finding someone else would take time. If nothing else, he could use it as a chance to prove that she meant absolutely nothing to him.

He eyed her, not agreeing just yet. 'Is taking your vows really worth crossing swords with me, little nun?'

Why are you thinking about her vows?

He had no idea.

She lifted one fair brow. 'I don't know. What's wearing a crown worth to you?'

A fair comment, and clearly time to leave.

'Very well,' he said. 'I shall expect a report every evening on Ione's progress and if her behaviour hasn't improved in two weeks' time

then you're going back to England with no argument.' He fixed her with a very level stare.
'Is that clear?'

'Yes, sire,' she said meekly enough.

But he didn't miss the tiny spark that lit in
her eyes.

He pretended not to notice.

CHAPTER THREE

ANNA BENT OVER her suitcase and dug through the limited items of clothing she'd brought with her, though what she was looking for she didn't know. She hadn't packed much, since she didn't have much and clothing had never been important to her, so why she wished she had something more than a couple of plain dresses in her suitcase, she couldn't fathom.

Tonight was her first meeting with the king to give her report on Ione and she wanted to wear something...different. For inexplicable reasons.

Perhaps it was nerves. She desperately hadn't wanted to return to England and him granting her two weeks to make some difference to Ione's behaviour had been a concession she hadn't been expecting. She'd argued for it, of course, but he'd been so adamant it had felt like hurling herself at a stone wall and expecting it to break.

Snapping at him had been a mistake, but all that seduction talk had irritated her.

It wasn't irritation you were feeling.

Anna scowled at the contents of her suitcase, not liking that thought one bit. She'd tried to ignore her own physical reaction to him, to ignore that he was half-naked, but then he'd started talking about how the Reverend Mother was meddling in his affairs—affairs apparently including her being sent to seduce him.

'You're round and soft and sweet. Just the kind of woman who would appeal to me.'

Heat crept through her, the way it had done all day whenever she'd thought of him saying those words, which she'd tried very hard *not* to do. Because they made her feel…strange.

He'd called her round, but it was obvious he hadn't meant it in a bad way. In fact, the opposite. *Just the kind of woman who would appeal to me…*

She felt even stranger when she thought about that; appealing to him had never occurred to her. In fact, appealing to anyone at all had never occurred to her. The sisters always discouraged such vanity. Some of the younger ones had giggled a bit over one of the better-looking priests, but Anna herself had never thought about men or her own desirability. Once or twice she'd wondered whether she might like a husband and a family, but then had dismissed the idea. Romantic relationships had seemed fraught and dangerous to her, while the relationships she had with the sisters at the convent were much less complicated. There were clear rules for behaviour and you didn't have to fit yourself around another person's needs and wants.

It was less exciting maybe, but at least life at the convent was a known quantity. At least, she fitted there better than she fitted anywhere else.

You still liked the fact that you appealed to him.

Anna scowled and pulled a dress out from the depths of her case. It was fancier than her other dresses, in a silky ice-blue fabric with a demure scooped neckline and capped sleeves. The colour was pretty on her—or at least that was what Sister Mary Alice had told her, and Sister Mary Alice was known to have good taste.

She didn't like that she appealed to him. Not at all. Round and soft and sweet, indeed. It made her sound pathetic and ineffectual and she didn't much appreciate that. Nor did she appreciate that the Reverend Mother had perhaps had an ulterior motive for sending her here, either. Certainly, she'd never mentioned seduction to Anna.

Not that she should be concerning herself with such things. The Reverend Mother clearly had a purpose in sending her here and it wasn't up to Anna to wonder at it. She had to trust that the Reverend Mother knew what she was doing.

Still, as she put the dress on, Anna found herself glancing in the full-length mirror at the foot of the bed and noticing that her breasts and hips and thighs were all soft and gently rounded.

Just the kind of woman who would appeal to me...

She pulled down the dress hurriedly and smoothed the fabric, ignoring the unexpected glow of warmth inside her. No, she didn't want to like that she appealed to him. Because, no matter what either the king or the Reverend Mother thought, she was here for Ione. And to show her obedience so she could take her vows.

Two weeks he'd allowed her. Two weeks to prove herself and hopefully not get sent home.

It wasn't much time in which to gain the trust of a child, let alone modify her own behaviour.

She'd made a start, though. Since she didn't know Ione and Ione didn't know her, Anna had decided to spend a couple of days on some getting-to-know-you activities. Today Anna had chosen drawing in the library for a nice, quiet activity that would allow some space to talk.

However, Ione hadn't been very interested in drawing—or, at least, not until Anna had had a brainwave and, remembering the girl's sword of the day before, had suggested drawing a knight fighting a dragon. That had gone very well until Ione had insisted on performing said fight and had knocked over a lamp that had been sitting on the table.

The little girl was a live wire, reminding Anna uncomfortably of herself when she'd been that age. It also made her wonder if some of the girl's boisterousness came from a lack of attention. She remembered feeling alone, as if she didn't fit in. There had been other children in the foster home run by the nuns and she'd made a few friends, but they never stayed very long, many of the other children having found homes.

But not Anna. No one had wanted to adopt her. And no wonder, since she'd always been over-loud, over-eager, over-friendly. Like a puppy, one of the sisters had said.

Perhaps that was the issue with Ione. Perhaps the little girl was lonely. It was something to raise with the king anyway.

She was sticking another pin into her bun when there was a knock on her door from a guard waiting outside to escort her to the king for her meeting.

Anna hadn't seen him since the day before, and as she followed the guard down the echoing stone corridors of the palace her pulse started to gather speed and her palms got sweaty, nervousness gathering inside her. All she could think about was him in the ring, moving fluidly around his opponent, the flex and release of hard muscle beneath olive skin, the way he'd stared at her, blue eyes piercing her...

Silly. She was silly. She wasn't a lovesick teenage girl and he wasn't a handsome teenage boy. He was a king, for goodness' sake.

The guard stopped in front of a heavy wooden door and Anna tried to moisten her dry mouth as he knocked and waited for admittance. The king's harsh voice called for them to enter, and then the door opened and she was ushered inside.

It was a large room with a stone floor and once again, like the whole palace, it seemed, the walls were of bare stone. Heavy wooden bookshelves stood against them, stacked with expensive-looking leather-bound books, while a massive wooden desk sat under one window. There was also a cavernous fireplace—unlit—with yet more heavy furniture in the form of a couch and an armchair arranged around it. Lamps were positioned at strategic points, giving the room a soft, diffused light, the bare stone softened with silk rugs on the floor and yet more dusty tapestries on the walls. The only concession to modernity seemed to be the sleek, paper-thin computer screen that sat on top of the huge desk.

The king himself was sitting behind the desk, looking at said screen, and for a second he looked so incongruous that Anna could only stare. She could imagine him on the battlefield wielding a sword, had literally seen him in the boxing ring throwing punches. But for some reason his sitting at a desk, frowning ferociously at a computer screen like an office worker, seemed…wrong somehow.

Then again, he sat in his office chair as if it were a throne, his authority and power a physical force radiating from him. His white business shirt was undone at the throat, the sleeves rolled up on his sinewy forearms, exposing his olive skin, and if he looked like anything at all, it was a *Fortune 500* CEO hard at work.

He didn't glance up as she entered the room and she was left to stand there awkwardly as the guard withdrew, closing the door behind him. The king frowned at the computer then hit a few keys, giving no hint that he was aware of her, which annoyed her intensely.

How did he do that? How did he make her feel as if she were once again the disobedient child sent to the Reverend Mother for punishment? She resented it, especially now that she was a grown woman and had left the disobedient child in her behind a long time ago.

Have you, though?

Anna bit her lip, forcing that thought away. True, she hadn't exactly been a model of good behaviour since she arrived in Axios, but she had far more control over herself than she had used to. Plus, she'd learned from her mistakes. She wouldn't let her irritation or impatience get to her. She would be calm and poised and obedient.

She managed to stand there without fidgeting for what she was sure was a good ten minutes before he finally looked up from the screen. She'd braced herself, yet still the impact of his sharp, cold gaze was enough to make her catch her breath.

'You may approach,' he said curtly.

Anna went over to the desk and stopped in front of it, clasping her hands together in front of her. He'd focused on her very intently, and she found herself blushing again.

You appeal to him.

Oh, but she didn't want that in her head, not with him staring at her like that, making a deep part of her shiver. And it definitely wasn't because she was cold.

He said nothing and the tension that she'd felt the day before in the gym coiled around them. It made her uncomfortable, so she opened her mouth to say something, anything, but he forestalled her.

'My daughter broke a lamp in the library

today.' His blue gaze was so sharp it was a wonder he hadn't drawn blood. 'You wouldn't happen to know anything about that, would you?'

Anna took a slow, silent breath. She'd known that would get back to him and she'd hoped it wouldn't annoy him. Sadly, that didn't seem to be the case.

'Oh, yes,' she said. 'I was, of course, going to mention that.'

'Were you indeed? Explain.'

There was a hard note in his harsh voice that made her bristle and she wasn't sure what it was about this man that got under her skin so badly, because it didn't make any sense. She behaved herself with the Reverend Mother and the other sisters; what was it about this king that made her want to push back at him?

'I thought it would be a good idea if we got to know each other first,' she said, holding on to her poise. 'So we did some drawing in the library. She wasn't much interested until I suggested she draw a knight fighting a dragon. And then she decided to re-enact it and, well… she got a little carried away.'

The king's expression could have been carved

out of granite. 'You're supposed to manage her behaviour.'

Anna tried to ignore her irritation at his curt manner. She didn't expect him to be friendly—it was clear from the two times she'd been in his presence before that friendly was the last thing he was—but he didn't need to be quite so rude.

'It's the first day,' she said, attempting calm. 'I needed to get to know her and she needed to get to know me.'

He said nothing, his gaze sharp as a knife.

'She's high-spirited,' Anna felt compelled to add. 'And if you ask me, she's probably also a little neglected.'

Instantly, the king's demeanour changed, the lines of his face hardening even more, his big, powerful body tensing. Deep in his icy blue eyes, real anger glowed.

'Be careful.' His deep voice vibrated with an edge of warning. 'Be very careful what you say about my daughter.'

Anna flushed, realising belatedly how she'd sounded. 'I don't mean she's neglected physically,' she said hurriedly. 'What I meant was that she might be acting up to get attention.'

The king's expression didn't soften. 'And you came to this conclusion how? Based on what? Your thorough and extensive knowledge of my daughter?'

Sarcasm edged every word, making her flush even deeper. She was digging herself a hole, and if she wasn't careful it would get so deep she wouldn't be able to climb out of it.

And then he'll send you home.

No. That was not going to happen.

She met his gaze with equanimity. 'No. Based on my own experience as a very lonely child.'

Adonis didn't want to ask her. He wasn't interested in her or her childhood. But she was standing in front of his desk, wearing a sweet little dress of pale blue that wasn't at all like the plain grey dress of the day before. The colour was lovely on her, highlighting her creamy skin and giving her grey eyes a blue tinge. But that wasn't the worst part. The worst part was that, though the dress had a very demure neckline, it hugged the curves of her breasts and moulded deliciously to her hips, before flaring outward in a silky-looking skirt. It was a cheap dress, yet it also highlighted the fact that this little nun had the most beautiful, womanly body.

Not that it was merely her body he found appealing. If only it had been, because then he wouldn't have had any issues. Lust could be controlled easily enough. No, it was the intriguing fire in her that added to his fascination. The hint of a rebellious spirit. It shouldn't attract him, since it was the antithesis of what he believed in himself, but he'd always liked a strong woman. And, for all that she seemed so sweet and innocent, there was more backbone to her than he'd first thought.

She definitely wasn't a quail or a rabbit, which made her a problem.

Ever since yesterday, when she'd demanded that he change his mind about sending her away, he hadn't been able to get her out of his head. All he'd thought about was that spark in her eyes as she'd snapped at him, the flush to her cheeks as he'd talked about seduction. The way she hadn't been able to stop looking at his body…

It had been inconvenient. He'd tried to busy himself with other things, but she'd remained stuck in his thoughts like a song that kept playing over and over again. He hadn't had a woman occupy so much of his thinking before and it was clear he was going to have to take steps to resolve the issue.

Perhaps telling her to meet with you every night was a mistake.

Perhaps, but the thought of not being able to stand even ten minutes of her company without being bothered was ludicrous.

Yet he was bothered now, irritated by his body's response to her and annoyed by her suggestion that Ione had been neglected. He shouldn't let either of those things touch him, but they did.

Ione was *not* neglected. She had everything a child could possibly need, and if she was acting up to get attention, then she needed to learn that was not acceptable. Immediately.

Adonis stared hard at the woman standing on the other side of his desk. A lonely childhood... He didn't care. His mother had been killed at the hands of enemies of the crown when he was seven, causing his father to start down the road of teaching Adonis about the importance of detachment. Lessons that had involved making him listen to his little brother's torture.

It had been a hard childhood but a necessary one. Loneliness, in comparison, was a walk in the park.

'Is that so?' he said, which wasn't what he'd meant to say at all.

'Yes.' She lifted her determined chin as if she was facing him down over something that really mattered instead of something as insignificant as a childhood long gone. 'My mother gave me up when I was a baby and I was brought up in a foster home run by the nuns. They weren't cruel or abusive, but they weren't exactly warm either. And they didn't much approve of high spirits or emotional outbursts.'

She said it very matter-of-factly, though there was a faint note of something else in her voice, something he couldn't immediately identify.

He sat back in his chair slowly, looking at her. He didn't care. He wasn't interested. Yet somehow his mind started down a track he didn't want it to, wondering how she'd come to be at the convent and whether she was a woman looking for an escape from modern life or following a family tradition. But neither of those things apparently; she said she'd been given up for fostering...

His detachment was perfect. His emotions were completely under his control. If he didn't want to feel anything, he didn't, and so there should have been no reason for a strange, unidentified feeling to coil in his chest. No reason for questions to suddenly occur to him, such as why she hadn't been wanted, and whether she'd been adopted at last. But no, she hadn't been adopted. If she'd been brought up by the nuns and was hoping to take her vows, then it was likely she'd remained in the foster home...

Why are you thinking these things?

It was a good question, especially when it made the unidentified sensation in his chest coil tighter.

He ignored it, annoyed at being made to feel anything at all. 'And? You have a point to this?'

'Of course I have a point.' She frowned. 'I don't give people I don't know well personal information about my childhood for the fun of it.'

You have offended her.

So? What did it matter? He didn't care about his own feelings, still less other people's. A king was supposed to rule with his head, not his heart.

Then again, offending people needlessly

wasn't diplomatic. Perhaps he should have got Xerxes to handle these interviews, since his brother was a lot more charming than he was.

If you can't deal with one small novice, perhaps your detachment isn't as perfect as you thought.

A cold sensation wound through him. No, he would not accept that. His father's lessons had been brutal ones, but he'd learned them. Emotions in a ruler were a threat and one he couldn't afford.

He had to do better.

'Continue.' He made an effort to keep the harshness of his temper from his voice.

She gave him a suspicious look then went on, 'As I was saying, the nuns were distant and not particularly loving, and I felt lonely. As a consequence, I got into trouble quite a lot, since being disobedient got me more attention than sticking to the rules.'

That was probably the least surprising thing she'd said all evening. Especially given that rebellious spark that showed in her eyes. In fact, he could just imagine her in a strict foster home, racing around with flushed cheeks and a loud voice, arguing with the nuns and perhaps stamping her foot...

Warmth curled through him, a warmth he didn't recognise. The same kind of warmth that had touched him when she'd smiled at him the day before. A spark flickering in the dead hearth of his heart.

He let it die. 'So you're saying my daughter is acting up to get attention?'

'Yes, that's exactly what I'm saying.'

'An interesting theory, but you're wrong.' He sat forward again, glancing down at the screen so he wouldn't have to look at her face, wouldn't feel the tug of curiosity that pulled at him, making him want to ask her more about how the nuns had treated her, why she'd felt so lonely, and more about the ways in which she'd been disobedient.

You could get her to be disobedient. Very disobedient...

'My daughter gets plenty of attention,' he went on, shoving that particular thought aside. 'She has many people who give her nothing but attention day in and day out. She's—'

'I believe she needs attention from you.'

Adonis blinked at his computer screen. This

was the second time in as many days that she'd interrupted him.

Then what she'd actually said penetrated.

Attention from him.

You can't give it.

No. At least not the kind of attention he thought Anna probably meant. He was not that kind of father. He was a king first and foremost, and everything else came second. Even his daughter. Already, he'd noticed that Ione was too much like he had been as a child. Wild and rowdy and demanding, her emotions all over the place, and he knew where that led. He had to make sure she didn't make the same mistakes he had.

Attention wouldn't cure that, only discipline could.

Adonis pushed his chair back and stood up, staring down at the little nun on the other side of his desk, knowing he was being deliberately intimidating and not caring. He would not have his decisions questioned, and certainly not by her. If she needed a lesson in respect, he would deliver one.

Her eyes widened as he stood, but she didn't lower her gaze. Didn't lower that insolent little chin either. She stood her ground, watching him as he stalked around the side of his desk, coming over to her and staring down at her from his far greater height.

'I suggest, Sister Anna, that you remember your place.' He didn't bother to soften his voice this time. 'If I wanted your opinions on how I parent my child then I would ask for them. But I do not. Seeing as how you are a childless, sheltered nun, I fail to see why you would think your opinions should matter to anyone at all.'

A dull flush crept over her cheeks, her lovely mouth hardening, the pulse at the base of her throat beating fast. He thought she might turn around and run away weeping, since that had been his late wife's response when he'd had occasion to lay down the law. Sophia had never been able to handle his coldness.

But Anna didn't burst into tears or run away. It was likely he'd hurt her, and if so then good, because she had to understand who she was dealing with. But he was also sure that the spark of pure silver that lit up in her gaze wasn't only hurt. It was temper as well.

Dangerous.

No, it wasn't dangerous. He wasn't in the

gym now; this was his office and he was in perfect control of himself, regardless of their chemistry.

She opened her mouth as if to speak, then shut it again, her hands at her sides and clenched into fists. It was clear that she was struggling with her temper. Taking a deep breath, the fabric of her dress pulling tight across those lovely breasts, she said, 'I'm not questioning your parenting decisions, and I'm sorry if it came across as if I were. But you wanted me to report every evening on the progress Ione is making and so here I am, giving you a report.'

Interesting that she'd managed to keep herself under control. Perversely, it made him want to push her harder, to test her mettle. She smelled of lavender, a prosaic, homey kind of scent, with something a little sweeter and muskier beneath it, and he found he didn't have it in him to step away just yet.

'A report is a factual account of the day's events, not your very under-qualified opinion,' he said implacably, watching the temper ebbing and flowing across her pretty face.

The spark in her eyes glowed hotter. 'I'm well aware of my lack of qualifications. You don't need to remind me. But I only want to do what's right for your daughter.'

She should back down, she really should. There could be no good outcome from standing up to him like this.

But you like it.

A part of him did. A part of him liked how she didn't back away, fascinated by the stubborn lift of her chin and the spark in her eyes.

He'd once felt things the way she did, deeply and passionately. But it was so long ago now, he barely remembered it.

'I know what's right for my daughter.' He held her gaze. 'Because I'm her father. You're a person she spent a couple of hours with and that's all.'

The flush in her cheeks became scarlet. 'You wanted me to help her and that's exactly what I'm doing. It's not my fault you don't like what I'm telling you.'

He shouldn't get any closer, but somehow he'd taken another step forward anyway, close enough to feel the heat her curvy little body was throwing out, see the lighter flecks in her eyes, making it seem as if they were shimmering.

Was she deliberately inciting him? It certainly felt like it. He'd told her to give him some respect twice now, and yet here she was, still talking back, having not listened to a thing he said. She hadn't learned her lesson. She hadn't learned it at all.

Why do you care whether she learns it or not? Isn't your control supposed to be perfect?

It was. But his patience wasn't limitless and everyone had a line. And she was innocent. She wouldn't understand what this kind of pushing did to a man like him. The man behind the king.

He hadn't thought of that man for a long, long time. He thought he'd crushed the remaining shreds of him the day Xerxes had been banished from Axios, the last vestiges of the selfish, out-of-control child he'd once been, who hadn't listened to what his father was trying to teach him. The rebellious teenager whose refusal to learn had got his brother hurt.

There shouldn't have been anything left of that man at all now.

Apparently, though, he was wrong. The man wasn't as dead as he'd first thought. He was still there and hungry for what he couldn't ever allow himself to have.

A pretty, sweet, innocent woman.

Then again, she wasn't so sweet, was she? She had a bite to her and he liked that. He liked that far too much.

'You'd better be careful what you say to me,' he murmured. 'I like a fight, little nun. And if you challenge me, I will answer it.'

Her jaw tightened. She looked furious. 'I'm just trying to—'

But Adonis had had enough. He lifted a hand and laid his finger across that pretty mouth. 'The hole you're in is getting deeper by the second. I suggest you stop digging.'

Her lips were soft against his skin and very warm, and her eyes had widened. It was a mistake to touch her and he knew that, but she wasn't listening to him and he had to get her to stop somehow.

Better a finger over her lips than his own mouth, which was what he wanted to put there.

Shock flickered over her face, the pulse at the base of her throat beating even faster.

He took his finger away, the warmth of her

mouth lingering on his skin. 'Have you finished?'

'Yes.' Her voice was thick and slightly unsteady.

'Then you may go.'

Her throat moved and for a second she stared at him as if she'd never seen him before in her entire life. Then she turned abruptly and walked to the door, flung it open, and went out.

And he was not disappointed about that. Not disappointed at all.

CHAPTER FOUR

ANNA PULLED THE ice-blue dress over her head again and smoothed it down once more. Then she took a breath and tried to calm herself. Her heartbeat was thumping loudly in her ears and the nervous flutter in her gut that happened whenever she thought of the king was fluttering even harder.

She didn't want to check her appearance in the mirror, because she wasn't supposed to care what she looked like. It wasn't supposed to matter that she was wearing the same dress for the second night in a row. Her clothing was unimportant.

What was important was that the afternoon she'd spent with Ione had gone well—or, at least, nothing had ended up being broken. She'd asked Ione to take her on a tour of the palace, chatting to the little girl as they went, and it soon became obvious that Ione worshipped her father. It was all 'Papa said this' and 'Papa said that'. But it was also plain that Papa was always very busy and didn't spend much time with his daughter.

Anna understood—a king was very busy. But she did wonder why it was that he couldn't take a couple of moments out of his day to chat to her, hug her, give her some praise, because it was clear that Ione was crying out for it.

She was a bright, sparky, emotional kid who was plainly lonely. And Anna knew how that felt. How it was possible to be surrounded by people all the time and yet still feel as if you were on your own.

It didn't help that after a bit of investigation, Anna discovered that the little girl had no friends her own age. Puzzled, she'd questioned the nanny about it, and the nanny had explained that the lack of friends was a security issue. Ione was the king's only heir and he protected her zealously.

The thought of Ione's loneliness made Anna's own heart sore and it cemented her decision to do what she could to help the little girl.

She thought about taking Ione into Itheus for ice cream, but after looking at the list of things she wasn't permitted to do, Anna soon realised that the princess wasn't allowed out of the palace without a contingent of guards in attendance, which severely limited her plans.

In fact, there seemed to be many things Ione wasn't permitted to do and Anna couldn't help wondering if those rules were all really necessary. She was such a sparky, intelligent kid and it was likely some of her behavioural issues weren't all to do with loneliness, but had a bit of boredom mixed in there as well.

Anna touched her hair nervously. Given how the king had reacted the night before, she was reluctant to bring these issues to his attention, but if she didn't speak up for Ione, then who would?

'I know what's right for Ione. I'm her father. You're a person she spent a couple of hours with, nothing more...'

A flare of volatile anger licked up inside her, but she fought it down. She couldn't lose her temper again the way she had the day before. She couldn't let the king get to her, no matter how rude or dismissive he was. She'd overstepped the mark and badly and he'd...

The memory of his finger on her mouth washed over her, the heat of his skin like a brand, and even now, nearly a whole day later, she could still feel the imprint of it against her lips. She'd never been touched by a man before anywhere, let alone on her mouth, and, since she had no idea how to handle it, she'd solved the issue by not thinking about it at all.

Except she couldn't help but think of it now, of him standing so close, towering like a mountain over her. She'd never been that close to a man before either and maybe she should have been afraid, because he'd made her suddenly aware of how much bigger he was than her and how much more powerful. Yet it hadn't been fear that had gripped her but anger. She'd been furious at him for dismissing her and what she had to say as if it didn't matter. As if he hadn't been the one to order her to report to him every night on his daughter's progress.

She might have been the one insisting on staying in Axios, but he'd wanted her to help with his daughter's behaviour and so she would. It was important. And spending more time with Ione only made her realise just how important.

The king had certain...thoughts about his role as a father, clearly, which being a king exacerbated. He certainly didn't like being told he was neglectful—which she hadn't meant at all—but she seemed to have hit a nerve when she'd mentioned that perhaps what Ione needed was his attention.

She'd have to go carefully and stay calm if she was going to tackle this.

And definitely do not think about him touching your mouth.

No, most especially not that.

The guard knocked on schedule and Anna gave her dress one last smooth down before following him along the echoing palace corridors to the king's office once again.

This time the king was in a meeting and Anna had to wait in the corridor outside until finally a group of people came out of the room, talking amongst themselves.

The king was standing in the middle of the room, looking down at a piece of paper he held in one hand and frowning at it. He wore plain, dark grey suit trousers and a dark blue shirt open at the neck, and again the sleeves were rolled up.

His roughly handsome blunt features were set in their usual granite lines, betraying absolutely nothing, and his posture was imposing, those broad shoulders giving no sign of weariness. Yet…she couldn't shake the impression that he was…tired somehow.

Perhaps she didn't need to bring her thoughts about Ione to him tonight. Perhaps she should just give him what he'd requested—a factual account of events—and leave it at that.

'Enter,' he said, not looking up as she came into the room.

The guard closed the door and silence descended as the king continued to read whatever was on that piece of paper.

Anna looked around, noticing that on the low table near the couch some refreshments had been laid out. Cheeses and olives and various different breads. A bottle of white wine, condensation beading the green glass, was standing next to the food, along with some glasses. It all looked untouched; obviously the meeting had been a serious one with no time for relaxation.

Without thinking, she went over to the coffee table, poured out a glass of the wine and came over to where he stood.

'Here,' she said, holding out the glass to him. 'You look like you could do with this.'

He looked up, surprise crossing his features as he glanced at the wine in her hand then back at her again. For a second she thought he might refuse, but then he reached for the glass and took it from her. 'Thank you.' His blue gaze was customarily sharp and cold, and she felt again the burn of his touch on her lips, sensitising her mouth and making her breath catch.

No, she shouldn't be thinking of that. Shouldn't be thinking about what he'd meant when he'd told her how he liked a fight. How if she challenged him he'd accept it. What would it mean to fight him? She didn't imagine he meant actual fighting and, given that there had been something flickering in the depths of his icy blue gaze, he'd probably meant...

You know what it means.

Heat stole through her and her skin prickled. She shouldn't be thinking about this, about *any* of this. She was here for Ione, first of all, and to do her duty to the Reverend Mother, second. She couldn't allow herself to be sidetracked by inappropriate thoughts.

'What was that for?' the king asked.

'The wine?' She lifted a shoulder. 'You looked like you needed it.'

His gaze narrowed, but he didn't say anything else, raising the glass to his lips and taking a sip. 'Your report, please.'

It looked as if he was in no mood for chit-chat, which was fine. It was probably a good idea not to spend too much time in his company anyway.

Anna straightened and gave him a brief run-down on what she and Ione had done. 'Nothing got broken today at least,' she said as she finished up. 'And tomorrow I'd like to take her into Itheus for some ice cream and maybe a visit to a playground.'

'I see.' The king looked down at his paper again, sipping absently at his glass of wine.

Anna briefly tossed up whether to mention she wanted to take Ione without her usual phalanx of guards or whether to tackle that issue tomorrow. Then again, if she wanted to take Ione without the guards, she'd need the king's approval and she might not be able to get it in time if she waited. She might as well ask him now, while he was here.

'I was thinking,' she began hesitantly, 'that it would be good to take her without a guard detail. Or at least not one so large.'

The king didn't even look up. 'No.'

Anna was conscious of the kick of her temper and firmed her grip on it. 'It wouldn't be for long,' she tried again. 'Just for an hour—'

'What part of no don't you understand?' He looked up from his paper, an icy glitter in his eyes. 'Ione will go nowhere without her guards.'

Last night his curt dismissal had irritated her unreasonably. Tonight though, for some reason, it didn't annoy her quite as much and she wasn't sure why. Perhaps it was because she sensed that there was something deeper going on here. He was tired, she knew that, and she could also sense his distraction. He clearly had a lot on his mind.

He was so hard and so powerful and so cold, and it was easy to assume that as a king he was somehow superhuman. He certainly looked it. Yet he wasn't. He was just a man, just a human being as she was.

'Is something wrong?' she asked before she could think better of it.

Surprise flickered across his features and then was gone. 'No. What makes you say that?'

'You just look…tired.'

He said nothing for a moment, then abruptly

turned and went over to his desk, putting the wine and the paper he'd been holding down on it. 'It's none of your concern. Is that all?'

His posture was very tense and she had the strangest impulse to go over to him and put a hand on his back, to ease the stiffness from him. It was very odd to feel such sympathy for him. Especially considering how arrogant and autocratic he was towards her.

Clasping her hands together instead, she said, 'No, not quite all. I didn't mean to take Ione without any guards at all. Perhaps just Hesta and one other. And the rest could—'

'Why?' he interrupted yet again, turning and pinning her in place with his cold blue stare. 'What is this insistence on taking her out of the palace?'

Irritation prickled over her skin at his tone, but she tried to stay calm. 'I thought she might like a change of scene.' And then, with sudden inspiration, added, 'She will be ruling this country at some point, so it might be interesting for her to see a bit more of the town at least, and the people who live there.'

He stared at her. 'Why do you want to leave her guard detail behind?'

'Because it's difficult to have a normal outing to get ice cream and perhaps play at a playground when you have a whole troop of guards following you around.'

'What do you mean, a normal outing?'

Anna took a breath. She would have to go carefully here. 'Ione is very…restricted. She spends all her time at the palace with a lot of adults. I thought she might like to spend some time doing things an ordinary child might enjoy. Ice cream, for example. Playing with children her own age…' Anna trailed off as the expression on the king's face turned forbidding.

'If you want ice cream, I'll have it organised,' he said flatly. 'And there are plenty of places in the palace she can play. She doesn't need to go to Itheus to do it.'

The prickle of irritation became more insistent. 'So, you don't let her go anywhere without her guards? Is that what you're saying?'

'She is the heir to the throne,' his gaze was wintry, 'as well as my daughter, and no, she doesn't go anywhere without her guards.'

'Like I've already said, I don't mean to go without any guards at all. But perhaps only—'

'No.'

The word was iron, with no room for argument, and it annoyed her. She understood that he wanted to look out for Ione's safety, but such a restricted childhood could end up being smothering, and limiting, as she knew herself.

She wanted to argue, but that hadn't ended well the night before and it probably wouldn't end well tonight either, and so she bit back her protest. 'Very well, Your Majesty,' she said instead, trying not to let her annoyance colour her voice.

Silence fell, the look on his face impenetrable.

'You're very annoyed with me,' he said, and it wasn't a question.

'No, of course I'm not—'

'You are. Don't deny it.'

Anna bit her lip. 'Very well, I am.'

'Yet you're not arguing with me.'

'Because you told me not to. Remember?'

Something leapt in his gaze, something hot beneath all that ice, and again she was conscious of him the way she'd been conscious of him the night before. Of how tall he was and how broad. How the fabric of his shirt pulled over the hard muscles of his chest and how the colour deepened the blue of his eyes. Of his warm, musky scent, filtered with a freshness that reminded her of sunlight and salt and the ocean, and which she found almost unbearably attractive.

He was so cold and hard and distant, and yet right now he seemed almost…touchable.

A shiver wound its way down her spine and it wasn't fear or dread or foreboding or cold. It was much worse than that. It was excitement.

Slowly, the king leaned back against his desk, the tension that had been in his posture dissipating. He put the heels of his hands on the desktop, strong fingers gripping the edge, his intense stare unwavering.

'I remember.' His voice had lowered, become impossibly deeper. 'Are you wanting that fight, little nun? Is that why you're looking at me that way?'

Her cheeks were hot, a forbidden, wicked heat winding its way through her. 'I'm not looking at you in any way,' she said, her voice sounding distant even to her own ears.

He tilted his head, the glitter in his eyes no

longer so icy. 'Are you not? Because that blush in your cheeks would seem to say otherwise.'

Her eyes widened, her hands half rising as if to touch those pretty red cheeks of hers, before dropping back down to her sides. She was in that blue dress again and, since she'd also worn it the night before, it was probably because she didn't have another. It was an issue. Mainly due to the fact that she looked so sweet and delectable in it.

She would look even sweeter and more delectable out of it.

His thoughts were very much out of line tonight and he should be reining them in. But right in this moment, he couldn't bring himself to do it.

All day something had been eating away at him—a kind of impatience. He wasn't sure where it had come from, since impatience was another thing he didn't feel in the normal scheme of things, so he'd tried not to pay attention to it. But it had tugged at him, making it difficult to concentrate on his duties, which was a serious issue. Ruling his country required his full attention and he could not afford to be distracted.

It had got exponentially worse in the meeting he'd just had with his councillors. He hadn't been able to focus and he'd felt tired, along with the unfamiliar need to get up and pace, to shake off the tension somehow. It was mystifying. He'd never been bored or uninterested at a meeting before, but he'd been both tonight, sitting there, irritated, wanting them gone so he could…

He hadn't been sure what. Go down to the gym and do a few rounds with the punching bag. Do some lengths of the pool. Run on the treadmill. Do something hard and physical to get rid of whatever this feeling was the way he normally did.

Then his councillors had gone and she had come into the room, and it had all become very, very clear to him. His tiredness had dropped away and along with it the impatience, and he realised that she'd been the one he'd been waiting for the whole time. Waiting for evening to come, waiting to hear her report on his daughter. Waiting so he could match wits with her, waiting to get her all pink and furious and watch her eyes spark with silver fire.

It was disturbing. His entire life was crafted specifically to have no such needs. No such… attachments. No one whose company he looked forward to being in, no one he enjoyed talking with. He would allow himself nothing that would distract him from the duty he'd been born for—that of ruling a country. Axios came first and foremost, and always would. He'd betrayed it once before because he'd put someone else above it, and he wouldn't willingly do so again.

One little novice nun should not have the power to distract him so badly.

Despite his determination not to, he'd been very angry about that, not helped by her insistence that she take Ione out of the palace, a suggestion he'd refused point blank. Ione could go nowhere without her entire guard detail because her safety was paramount, and most especially if it involved going down into the city. Ice cream and playgrounds were also indulgent and he didn't like the thought of that either.

His refusal to even entertain the idea should have signalled the end of the meeting and then he should have sent Anna away. But he hadn't sent her away. Because she was standing there, all scarlet-cheeked and angry, that silver fire glittering in her eyes, making a very male satisfaction coil tightly inside him.

He wasn't impatient or tense any longer. He wanted to push her further, make her even more furious, see what she'd do, and that was very, *very* wrong of him. The king should send her away and put her from his mind, but the man refused. The man wanted her to stay. The man hadn't indulged himself in anything quite as sweet and innocent as she was, perhaps ever, and he wanted to hold on to this moment for as long as he possibly could.

Or hold on to her.

Yes, he did want to hold on to her. His hands itched to get rid of the cheap fabric of her dress and touch her silky skin, trace her softly rounded curves. Watch her eyes darken with desire, teach her exactly how good that beautiful body of hers could make her feel.

He gripped hard to the edge of the desk he leaned against. The man might want those things, but it was the king who remained in charge and it was the king who would continue to do so. He wouldn't touch her, no matter how much his body demanded otherwise.

Flirting with her would be a test of his control, but perhaps his control could do with a test. It had been a long time since he'd felt the need to, after all.

'I don't know what you're talking about,' the little nun said, all flushed dignity and poise.

He almost smiled. 'Then why are you blushing?'

Her mouth firmed. 'If you're talking about last night when you touched me, then of course I'm going to blush. You shouldn't have done that.'

'No,' he agreed. 'I shouldn't. And maybe I should send you away before I do it again.'

Her eyes widened and she didn't move. And for a moment the tension between them pulled tight, a humming vibration that set all his nerves alight.

It had been too long since he'd felt an attraction like this, far too long. And yes, he should send her away, but what harm would it do if he indulged himself for a moment or two? It was only physical chemistry, nothing more.

Good God, if he could send his own brother

into exile for ten years without a break in his heartbeat, then he could withstand the temptation of one small nun.

Are you sure about that?

Of course he was sure. Once, he might have been drawn to her rebellious spirit, his innate protectiveness might have been touched by her innocence and vulnerability. But not now. He was protective still, but that didn't focus on a person these days. It extended to an entire country.

It had taken more than his mother's death to teach him that lesson—he'd been a recalcitrant student—but he'd learned in the end.

'I don't understand,' she said, breaking the tense silence. She was standing very straight, her back flat, her chin lifted.

'I think you do.' He held her shocked gaze with his. 'You might be innocent, but you're not completely unworldly.'

The expression on her face shifted. 'I see. Is this something to do with the Reverend Mother sending me to you for seduction?'

She said the words with no hint of a stutter, but her hands had clenched tightly at her sides. Was it fear? Had he frightened her? Then again, he knew what fear looked like; he saw it in the eyes of people who faced him every day, and there was nothing of fear in hers. Only the flickering, leaping silver flame of her temper.

'She's very interested in my emotional welfare,' he said. 'She thinks I should marry again and has been suggesting eligible women as potential wives to me for months. And then you arrive, all innocent and sweet and unsuspecting. I knew what she was doing even if you didn't.'

She frowned. 'I'm not innocent and I'm certainly not sweet, so could you please stop saying that I am?'

Physical desire shifted and turned inside him. He wanted to push himself away from his desk and go to her, stand very close and look down into her silvery eyes, watch them darken. To see what would happen if he put himself within reach. Would she touch him? Would she have the courage? Perhaps he should find out.

'You're both of those things, little nun. Because if you weren't, you wouldn't be blushing quite so hard right now.'

She stared at him and he could feel that humming tension between them ratchet higher. He shouldn't be provoking her, yet he couldn't bring himself to send her away.

Suddenly she moved, coming right up to stand in front of him, and even though he was leaning back against his desk, he still had to look down at her.

Her gaze was very level, but her cheeks were bright red, her hands in fists. 'I'm not here to seduce you, Your Majesty,' she said flatly, 'whatever you or the Reverend Mother might think. So if that's what you're worried about, you needn't be.'

She smelled of that sexy combination of lavender and musk, and he could see that the blush had crept down her neck, disappearing beneath the demure neckline of her dress. How far did it go? All the way over those pretty breasts?

He shouldn't be curious. He shouldn't want to know.

The pulse at the base of her throat was beating very fast and her breathing had quickened. Not fear, no. She wasn't afraid, of that he was certain.

'I'm not worried, believe me,' he said, and then, because he couldn't help it, he added, 'But aren't you curious? Aren't you curious to see whether or not you could seduce me? How you, an innocent novice nun, could seduce a king?'

Her mouth opened, then shut again. Her knuckles were white as her hands clenched tighter, and he wasn't sure whether it was because she was holding herself back or whether she was angered by his suggestion.

It was a mistake to have said that and he knew it, but he wanted to see what she would do, and besides, it had been a while since he'd indulged in flirtation.

You want her to do more than flirt. You want her to touch you.

The thought wound seductively through his head. He couldn't deny that he did want that. But still, she was an innocent and under his protection, not to mention one of his own godmother's novices. She was also employed by him. All very good reasons why he shouldn't be encouraging her...

'No,' she said tightly. 'I'm not interested.'

Except her gaze didn't move from his, as if she was mesmerised.

'Perhaps you're not.' Why was he so tense? Holding himself so still? It was almost as if he didn't trust himself to move. 'Or perhaps you're just scared.'

'I'm not scared either.' She drew herself up even straighter. 'And you should stop manipulating me.'

Of course she saw through him. She wasn't stupid.

'Am I manipulating you? Or are you letting me?' He tightened his grip on the edge of the desk. 'Maybe I should dismiss you, little nun. Put us both out of our misery.'

It would have been better for her if she'd nodded her head and said nothing. If she'd waited for him to dismiss her. But she didn't. Instead, her gaze searched his. 'What misery?'

'The misery of wanting to touch a woman I shouldn't.' He regretted it as soon as the words left his mouth, because he never explained himself to anyone and he didn't know why he was doing so now. Not that he planned on doing anything about it, but still.

Then again, it was too late to take it back now. She knew.

'Oh.' She blinked as if in shock, the light catching the soft gold of her lashes.

'You're surprised?' His own heartbeat started

to accelerate, a dark, intense hunger collecting inside him. 'What about? I did tell you that you appealed to me.'

'I know, but…' She stopped, taking a ragged-sounding breath, staring hard at him. 'No one has ever said things like that to me before.'

Of course they wouldn't have. In a convent she would have been kept away from such concerns.

'Does it shock you?' He shifted, noting how she tracked the movement, like a prey animal watching a predator. Except this particular prey animal looked just as hungry as the predator himself.

The Reverend Mother would be appalled.

She would. But only if he did something about it, and he wasn't going to. They were only talking and talking wouldn't hurt. Neither would a bit of honesty. The king was still entirely in control.

'No,' she said slowly, as if she'd only just decided. 'No, it doesn't.'

'It should. I'm not the right man for someone like you.'

If you really thought that, she wouldn't still be standing here.

No, she definitely wouldn't.

'Someone like me,' she echoed, her forehead creasing. 'What does that mean?'

'Isn't it obvious? You've been brought up by nuns and you're intending to take your vows. You're inexperienced. Innocent. Sweet. Kind. And I am none of those things.'

She frowned. 'Just because I've been living in a convent doesn't mean I don't know anything about…s-sex.'

The way she stumbled over the word went straight to his groin, making the hungry thing inside him growl. Making him want to cross the space between them, rip away that dress, and show her exactly what she didn't know about sex.

Enough. Finish playing with her and send her away.

Yes, that was exactly what he should do. This had gone on long enough and, though his control was excellent, it was not limitless. It was time to call a halt before he did something he'd regret.

'If you can't even say the word without stuttering then you really don't know,' he said, pushing himself away from the desk and straightening. 'It's time to go, Sister Anna. I would leave now, while you can.'

CHAPTER FIVE

THE HEAT IN the king's piercing blue eyes was still there, but the aching, breathless tension that had stretched between them, that had surrounded his taut, powerful figure as he'd leaned against the desk, was starting to drain away.

Anna knew she should be glad of it, but she wasn't.

Every nerve-ending in her body had seemed to come awake as he stared at her, as he talked about seduction and sex, and about wanting to touch her.

He'd mentioned before that she appealed to him, but not quite in so blatant a fashion. And it made her feel hot, turning the flutter inside her into an electric, thrilling excitement. Making her wonder whether a novice nun, with no experience whatsoever of men, really could seduce a cold, hard king.

She shouldn't be thinking such things. And

if she'd really been the good, obedient servant of God she was trying to be, then she'd have told him in no uncertain terms not to speak to her like that. Then she'd have turned and walked out.

Yet she'd done none of those things. She'd found her gaze pinned by the electric blue of his, her awareness stretching out, taking in every inch of his muscular figure and how he leaned against the desk, the sinews in his forearms corded, the fabric of his trousers stretched over powerful thighs. His shirt was open at the throat and her mouth had gone dry for some inexplicable reason at the sight of his bare olive skin and the strong, steady beat of his pulse.

She was attracted to him; she was aware of that now in a way she hadn't been before. She was thinking forbidden thoughts. Such as how he didn't seem cold now or distant, but hot and so very close. What would happen if she got closer? What would he do? He'd told her he couldn't touch her, and all the reasons he'd listed were very good reasons.

But what about her? She shouldn't touch him, of course she shouldn't. He was a king and she was only a novice, not even a nun. He was also the father of her charge, which made him her boss.

But if what he said was true about the Reverend Mother, then perhaps seducing him is part of your brief.

The thought was so sharp and burning it seared itself into her brain.

He perhaps couldn't touch her, but she could touch him, couldn't she? It might even be what the Reverend Mother wanted her to do. Of course, the Reverend Mother would never have said such a thing out loud, if what he'd said about her was true...

These are all justifications. You just want to touch him.

Her breath came faster now, her skin sensitised. She knew nothing very much about sex, still less about men, but yes, it was true. She did want to touch him. She very much did not want to be dismissed.

'But,' she began huskily, 'I don't want to leave.'

He was very still, a great stone carving of a warrior with burning sapphires for eyes. 'Perhaps you didn't understand me.' His deep, harsh voice sounded rough, as if he was talking through a mouthful of gravel. 'Would you like me to be clearer?'

'No, I understood.' She'd taken a step before she was even conscious of doing so. 'I just don't want to go.'

His gaze turned hot and that tension was back again, like a wire stretched to vibrating point between them. 'And yet I suggest that you do.'

'A suggestion isn't an order.' She took another slow step, her heartbeat sounding louder in her head. 'And I'm not very good at taking orders either.'

'What are you thinking, little nun?' His voice was even deeper, a growl.

'I'm thinking, what if it was true?' Another step took her to stand right in front of him, her head tipping back so she could meet his searing blue gaze. 'What if a novice really could seduce a king?'

Then, before she could think better of it, she put her hand out and laid her palm on his chest.

The look in his eyes flared with a heat that took her breath away. Or maybe it was the heat of his body that did that, seeping through the cotton of his shirt and into her palm, making her feel as if she'd put her hand against a hot stove.

She'd never touched a man before. Were they all this hot or was it just him? And were they all this hard? Because he certainly was. He was hard as iron, but warm, like living rock.

All the air had escaped her lungs and what little there was around her all smelled like him, salt and sunlight and a musky, masculine scent that set her heart racing.

'You really shouldn't do that.' His voice was so deep she could feel the vibration of it against her palm.

She searched his blunt, handsome face, noting the muscle that leapt in the side of his jaw and the tightness around his eyes and mouth. He was so powerful, so in control, and yet he didn't look that way now. He looked pushed to the edge. Was that her affecting him so badly? Did she, with her lack of experience and lack of knowledge, really have power over him in this way?

The idea fascinated her. She'd always been at everyone else's beck and call, the foster child taken in and cared for not by choice, but by necessity. Her place at the convent had always felt as though it had to be earned by being quiet and good and obedient. It wasn't hers by right or birth. Even leaving the convent and coming to Axios had been at the Reverend Mother's behest. And she was only staying on his sufferance.

He had the power, yet right now, with her hand on his chest, it felt as if she had some too. A different kind of power, but power all the same.

She liked it. She wanted more.

'Why not?' she asked, her voice sounding even huskier. 'You said you couldn't touch me, but you didn't say anything about me touching you.'

His blue gaze was so hot, spearing her right through. 'And what do you think is going to happen? That I'm just going to stand here and let you touch me? And what about after that? Do you think I'll wait until you've finished and then let you walk away?'

Something trembled deep inside her. No, she hadn't thought about any of those things. She'd just…touched him, responding to an urge she hadn't been able to deny or contain.

'I don't know.' She swallowed, the heat of

his body burning into her. 'I haven't done this before.'

'I know you haven't. Which is why I suggested that you leave, because if you'd thought it through, you'd never have touched me.'

The trembling inside her got deeper, wider, and it wasn't fear. She wasn't afraid of him in the slightest; no, it was something else entirely.

'Why?' she asked. 'What would you do?'

He was very still for a second. Then he said, 'This.'

And before she could move, he reached out and pushed the fingers of one hand into her hair, then bent his head and covered her mouth with his.

She'd never been kissed before. Never had another person's mouth on hers. There had been the brief, dry blessings on her forehead from the nuns, but nothing more. She'd never had heat, the firm press of warm lips on hers, never had anyone cradle the back of her head the way he was doing now, so very gently. As if he was holding something precious.

Her eyes pricked in a sudden rush of hot tears. Because she would have said that before this moment she'd never imagined being kissed.

That she didn't want to be and never had. But that was a lie.

Everything she'd told herself was a complete and utter lie.

She *did* want it. And she *had* imagined it. But she'd told herself it wasn't something she could ever have so she'd shoved those thoughts away hard and pretended that such a thing had never occurred to her. Except now he was here and his mouth was on hers and the kiss was consuming her, making her aware of everything she'd never had, everything she told herself wasn't permitted.

And she wanted it. She wanted it *all.*

She put both hands on his chest, taking his heat and hard strength for herself, then she rose up on her toes, opening her mouth to him. He tasted hot, but with a cool bite from the wine he'd been drinking, and it was delicious. She wanted to drink from him.

A soft moan escaped her as the kiss deepened and he began to explore her mouth with his tongue and his teeth, tasting her as she was tasting him, sipping gently from her, giving her gentle nips, testing her with his tongue.

Her fingers closed, gripping the warm cotton of his shirt, even as she felt his hand close around her hair as if in answer. The tug on it felt so good, small bolts of sensation that made her breath catch—what little breath she had left. Which wasn't much. He was taking it all, but she didn't care. She'd give it all to him. Everything he wanted, she would give.

It felt as if she'd been waiting for this moment, for him, her entire life.

'Little nun,' he whispered roughly against her mouth. 'Anna. We must stop.'

No, she didn't want to stop. She wanted to keep going, to have him kissing her, holding her, to have the extraordinary heat and hard press of his body against hers for as long as she could stand it. To have the sense of loneliness that had always dogged her become muted and dull beneath his astonishing kiss.

She clung on, seeking his mouth, trying to follow him as he lifted his head, only to be brought up short by the grip he had on her hair.

The blue of his eyes was electric, blazing with heat, but there was only iron in his voice when he spoke. 'We have to stop. We can't do this.'

'Why not?' Her voice was husky and a little

raw, and she couldn't make her hands work, her fingers keeping their grip on his shirt.

The flame in his eyes burned everywhere it touched. 'So many reasons.'

'I don't care.' Her throat closed. She didn't want to give him up. Didn't want to lose this sense of connection, this feeling of closeness with another person. No, not just with another person, with him. 'Please, sire.'

'Anna...'

'I want you.' She couldn't hide her desperation. Didn't want to hide it from him. She wanted him to know what this meant to her. 'Please. I need...this. I need you.'

The blunt lines of his face were no longer expressionless but taut and sharp. As sharp as the blue of his eyes, relentless and fierce. 'You don't know what you're asking for.'

'Then show me.' She leaned into him, finally releasing the hold she had on his shirt, spreading her hands out on the hard warmth of his chest, pressing into it, loving the feel of him under her palms. 'Please, sire.'

He muttered a curse under his breath, a rough sound that echoed through her. His body tensed, his muscles tight, and she wanted to run her hands over him, to soothe him. Did he have anyone to do that for him? Did he have anyone to ease that tension? That tiredness she'd seen in him… Did he have anyone who gave him pleasure?

He probably has hundreds of women, you fool. He's a king. He could have anyone he wanted.

Yes, but he wasn't with just anyone now. He was with her. And it was her hair he had his hand in, her hands on his chest. And it was her he was looking at.

'You're a virgin,' he said. 'You'll be taking your vows. You're under my protection. Taking you like this, now, would be a violation of all those things.'

'I don't care.' And she meant it. She couldn't bear the thought of him letting her go and stepping away. All his heat withdrawing and all his strength, like a tide going out, leaving her high and dry. And lonely. Always lonely. 'I want you so much.' Her throat closed with the force of her emotion and she tried to swallow it down, realising belatedly that perhaps revealing herself so openly was a bad idea.

But perhaps he knew anyway, because his

other hand cupped her cheek. For all his massive strength he was gentle, his big palm so warm and reassuring that she wanted to weep. 'Anna.' He said her name huskily, the sound of it whispering over her, the expression on his face softening just a fraction. 'You will care. When it's over, you'll care very much.'

Her heart felt full, pushing against her ribs, each beat painful. 'Don't tell me how I'm going to feel. You don't know. I've never had this before. Never felt it before. And yes, I'll be taking my vows, but I don't need to be a virgin to take them.'

Some emotion she didn't understand flickered over his face. 'And how will you feel afterwards? When I pretend it never happened? That none of this did? When you go back to being my daughter's companion and a trainee nun? Because that's what will happen. You can't be my lover, not openly, not given my position, and that's to protect both of our reputations. I will not acknowledge you as anything more than my daughter's companion and one of my godmother's charges. My job is to protect people and that includes you.'

She understood and it all made perfect sense.

Of course he wouldn't be able to acknowledge her, just as she wouldn't be able to acknowledge him. He had a position to protect just as she did, and a country to lead.

'I understand,' she said thickly. 'I really do.'

'Do you?' His voice had become harsh. 'I have a duty to my country. If word got out that we were lovers, it would reflect very badly on both of us. I cannot be seen as a man who took advantage of someone weaker and more vulnerable, and that's how people would view it. And those that don't would look at you with suspicion. They would view you as a gold-digger or worse.'

She took a little breath as the implications sank in, because no, she hadn't thought of any of that. But again, it made sense. And it did nothing to calm either the desperation or the hunger inside her.

Except…he had much to lose. More than she did. If it got out that she'd had a king for a lover, the worst that would happen would be disappointment from the nuns and from the Reverend Mother. But for him, with a country to lead…

Her gut lurched. She couldn't ask it of him.

It was wrong of her. She didn't care about the nuns' disappointment in her—they were always disappointed in her—not when all she could think about was him.

She swallowed the bitterness that collected in the back of her throat at the unfairness of it all. 'Okay. I wouldn't want to put you in a bad position. I'm sorry. I should have—'

His hand in her hair tightened, cutting her off, his blue eyes blazing. 'I didn't say no.'

Everything in her went still and quiet.

Keeping his gaze on hers, he lowered his hand from her cheek, dropping it down to the small of her back and settling it there, heavy and sure. Then he eased her closer, fitting every inch of her up against every inch of him.

The heat between them was searing, burning her, but she didn't want to pull away. No, she only wanted to get closer, press harder against him, take more, take it all… 'What are you doing?' she asked breathlessly. 'I thought you said—'

'I know I did. And all of that is true. I want you to understand the implications and the consequences.' He eased her even closer, so her hips were pressed to his and she could feel the long, hard ridge of his arousal. 'Because I want you, little nun. I want you very badly. And you need to decide if you still want to go through with this, because if you don't, you need to tell me now and tell me very clearly, so there can be no doubt.'

He felt so good, hard and hot, and so strong. She wanted to surround herself with that heat, with his power and strength, have him burn out the loneliness that sat inside her, melt the ice in the centre of her heart.

She understood the implications, and the consequences, and even though a part of her knew that she didn't, not really, she found she didn't care. She wanted him. She wanted this moment, because she knew she'd never have it again. If she turned her back and walked out of that door, she would lose something precious and she would never get it back.

So she didn't think and she didn't hesitate. She simply slid her hands up his broad chest and around his neck, rose up on her toes, and claimed his mouth, giving him her answer.

She tasted exactly the way he'd thought she would. No, better. If that was even possible.

Sweet, like strawberries on a summer's day, or the fizz of very good champagne, the bubbles bursting on his tongue. Sweet, yes, but with the most delicious bite.

He shouldn't have kissed her, shouldn't have let her touch him. Because the moment she had, he knew he wouldn't be able to let her go. Definitely, he should have stopped himself from teasing her, taunting her, or daring her into challenging him.

But he'd never thought she would want him so badly, that she'd hold tight to him, her mouth hungry under his. He'd never expected that there would be tears in her eyes as he tried to put her from him, looking at him as if she were dying and he were her last chance of rescue. And he'd never realised that all of those things would get through his defences the way they had, making his control feel as tenuous as smoke, silently slipping through his fingers.

That could not be allowed. He had to get it back again and there was only one way to do that.

As if any of this is about your control. You just want her.

But he shoved those thoughts away. They

didn't matter right now, because her mouth was on his and she tasted hot and it had been a long time, such a very long time, since he'd had a kiss this sweet. This tantalising and delicious.

Her body against his was soft and warm, a musky feminine scent winding around him and he was so hard he ached. He mostly preferred his women toned and athletic, because he was a hard man, and demanding. But she was all softness and womanly curves, and he wanted to sink into her, take all that sweetness for himself.

He pushed his fingers further into her hair, the little bun at her nape unwinding, spilling silk all over his skin as he held her steady to take the kiss deeper. She made another of those little throaty moans, pressing delicately against him as she tried to kiss him back. Her tongue was hesitant at first and then got bolder, exploring him as much as he was exploring her.

If he wasn't careful, this inexperienced, sheltered little nun would undo him.

He shifted, picking her up in his arms and carrying her over to the long leather couch. Then he sat down on it with her in his lap. Her hair was hanging down her back, pale as moonlight over her skin, and she kept trying to kiss him, her breathing out of control and ragged in the silence of the room.

He ran his hands down her back, soothing her at the same time as he found the zip on her dress and gently tugged it down. She sighed as the fabric loosened around her, her mouth on his becoming even more hungry, her hands going to the buttons on his shirt and fumbling with them. But he was faster, easing the material off her shoulders. Then he touched her, stroking his hands beneath her dress and over her skin, and yes, she was exactly as silky and soft as he'd expected. She gasped against his mouth, shuddering delightfully under his touch as he found the catch of her bra and undid it. A sigh escaped her and she gave a little moan as he trailed his fingers down the length of her spine. There was no hesitation to her, no alarm. It was as if she trusted him implicitly, and that made another unfamiliar sensation tighten in his chest.

You have been nothing but hard and rude to her. Yet she trusts you...

How strange that that should…affect him, especially when he accepted the trust of a nation as his due. But there was something about her that awoke the protector in him. Even though he didn't concern himself with other people's feelings, he wanted to keep her safe, to give her the pleasure she deserved. A pleasure to remember when she left.

Keep your distance.

Ah, but this was a single sexual encounter. Making sure it was good for one inexperienced nun wouldn't compromise that. He could afford to take care.

So he controlled the hunger in himself, put a leash on it. And he merely sat with her in his lap, kissing her lazily, stroking her back up and down, getting her used to his touch. She took what he gave her and then shifted, her hands moving again to his shirt and fumbling with the buttons once more.

It was difficult to hold back, to let her undo those buttons and just sit there as she uncovered him with shaking hands. But he didn't want to frighten her and, since he was the one with the better control, he let her set the pace initially. Plus, it felt almost too good when she finally managed to undo his shirt, to have her cool fingers on his skin, tracing the muscles of his chest and abdomen. She looked mesmerised by him and he let her touch, let her explore. But then she leaned forward and kissed his throat, her mouth hot, and the control he thought he had handled suddenly dissolved.

He shifted one hand into her hair and pulled her gently away. He had to redirect this otherwise it might be over before it even began.

'Lift your arms for me,' he ordered quietly.

She didn't hesitate, obeying without a word, allowing him to ease her dress up and over her head, taking her bra with it so she was sitting on him, facing him, naked but for a pair of white cotton briefs.

His breath caught. She was so lovely. Her hair was a skein of pale gold lying across one shoulder, her eyes darkening into tarnished silver. The flush that had tinged her cheeks did indeed go all the way down, across her neck and chest, over the most perfect round breasts he had ever seen, and sweet pink nipples, ready for his touch. She didn't cover herself and she didn't look shocked as he stared at her, only looked back at him as if she liked him looking at her as much as he liked looking.

He slid one hand to the small of her back,

spreading his palm out, cradling her as he urged her forward once more, tasting the sweetness of her mouth. Then he eased his other hand to her hip, trailing his fingers up her silky warm skin, feeling her shiver, and he went higher and higher, until he found the curve of one full breast.

She gasped against his mouth, her body arching as he cupped her breast gently, then she moaned as he circled her nipple with his thumb, making her tremble.

'Oh…' The word was soft with wonderment and surprised delight. 'Oh…*sire*…'

'Call me by my name,' he murmured, rubbing his thumb over the sensitive tip of her breast, making her shudder yet again. 'I'm not a king right now.'

She sighed, arching into his hand, holding back nothing from him. 'Adonis…' His name sounded like a prayer, and he wanted to hear her say it again, so he ran his thumb over her nipple once more. And she obliged him, his name coming out sweetly husky.

The sound shivered through him and he couldn't remember the last time a woman had called him that, with no deference. Only a plea, a cry for more.

So he gave it to her, stroking her breast, toying gently with her nipple as he kissed her, exploring her mouth. And then, when she was panting, he eased her back across his arm and then it was his turn to put his lips to her throat, to taste the salty-sweet flavour of her skin.

She trembled, her pulse frantic against his tongue. But he held her still, going slowly as he trailed kisses over the delicate architecture of her collarbones, then further down, to the swell of those beautiful breasts, tracing the curves with his lips, before moving on to one hard nipple. He teased it, circling it with his tongue, which made her gasp his name yet again. Then he took it into his mouth, holding her as he sucked gently on it.

A moan escaped her, throaty and soft, and her hands lifted to his shoulders, gripping on to him. 'Adonis…oh…please…'

She smelled like sex and she tasted like heaven, and she was so warm, so soft and sweet. And he hadn't realised those were things he'd been craving, not until now.

His life was so very cold, nothing but hard

edges and sharp decisions, and she felt like the antithesis of that. He wanted more, to spend longer tasting every inch of her delectable body, to take his time, because these moments they had together wouldn't last.

He could only give her now. But that was probably a good thing. Already he was so hard he ached, and the way she was giving herself to him, nothing held back and so trusting… It could become addictive if he let it.

So, you'd better not let it, had you?

Oh, he wouldn't, no fear of that. She might push his physical control, but that was all. She didn't affect any other part of him, least of all the distance he kept between himself and the world.

This was sex. Nothing more.

He switched his attention to her other breast, sliding one hand from her hip down to her thigh and stroking gently, before moving inward and up, then between.

She went very still as his fingers brushed over the damp fabric of her knickers, stroking the heat and softness behind the cotton, and he heard her breath escape in a wild rush.

'Oh, yes,' she gasped, her whole body suddenly shaking. 'Oh, yes, *please...*'

There was such delight in her voice and so much desperation that he tightened his arm around her, drawing her in close so her bare breasts were against his chest, her silky skin and hard little nipples rubbing against him. Then he stretched out his fingers between her thighs, stroking her over the material of her knickers, making her gasp and squirm and wriggle against him.

'Do you want more?' he demanded, his own voice so rough it didn't sound like his. 'Is that what you want? More of me touching you?'

'Yes,' she gasped. 'Please...yes...'

So he hooked one finger into the fabric and pulled it aside, baring her. Then he stroked his fingertips through the soft little nest of curls between her thighs, the folds of her sex hot and wet just for him.

She moaned, her hands gripping tight to his shoulders, as if she would fall if she let go, her breathing coming in short pants. Her hips twisted, following his hand as he caressed her, teasing and stroking the most sensitive parts of her.

He'd thought she might be modest or perhaps a little shy, but she wasn't. Like a person dying of heat exhaustion in the desert finally finding an oasis, she threw herself into it, clothes and all.

It was incredibly gratifying.

He found himself kissing her lovely mouth harder and with more demand despite the fact that he'd told himself he was going to take this slow. And then he was testing the entrance to her body gently, pushing one finger into her slickness, feeling the incredible heat of her sex close around him.

She shuddered like a tree in a hurricane, her mouth turning as hungry and as demanding as he was, her hips shifting on his lap as if she was trying to find some relief. But there would be no relief for her. None but what he gave her.

'Adonis,' she said hoarsely, her fingers digging hard into his shoulders. 'Please… I need… I can't…'

He wanted to push her down onto the couch cushions, take her hard and immediately. But she wasn't experienced and this was new to her, and he didn't like the thought of taking her roughly, with no niceties at all. He wanted this to be good for her. He wanted her to remember it. Remember him.

Why should you care about that?

He didn't know. She wasn't a politician or one of his council. Not one of his generals or a fellow head of state. She was only one little nun with whom he happened to have some chemistry and there was no need at all for her to remember him.

But he wanted her to.

She was shaking in his arms now, moaning against his mouth, so he kept his hand between her thighs, his finger sliding in a rhythm that made her shake even harder. Then he pressed down on the most sensitive part of her with his thumb, just a small brush.

And he held her as she convulsed against him, a cry of pleasure escaping as the orgasm washed over her.

He let her sit there for a moment, running one hand absently up and down her back to ease her down, barely aware he was even doing it. It was painful having her in his lap because he was so hard. But he didn't move. There was something sweet about holding her in his arms, about the way she turned her hot face into his neck, her breath warm on his skin.

Then quite suddenly she sat up, her silvery eyes staring fixedly at him, a crease between her fair brows. She didn't seem concerned that she was sitting there basically naked while he was mostly fully dressed.

'Please tell me there's more,' she said, her voice scratchy.

And he found himself smiling, predatory and hungry.

'Oh, yes,' he murmured, impatient now. 'There's more.' Then he moved, taking her down onto the couch beneath him. 'There's a lot more.'

CHAPTER SIX

ANNA FELT AS if she was outside herself. As if she'd changed in some way, become someone else. Someone who didn't have to be quiet and good. Someone who didn't have to make sure she was grateful all the time for any scrap of attention that came her way.

She'd become a woman made entirely out of heat and sensation, a wanton who demanded attention and got it. Who demanded pleasure and got it.

Who had the entire focus of the most beautiful, most exciting, most powerful man in the world centred on her and her pleasure.

She lay on the couch, the leather cool against her back, with Adonis's big, hard body stretched above her, and there was nowhere on earth she wanted to be right now other than where she was, beneath him.

She'd had no conception of what sex could be like. What touch could mean. Had no idea that she wouldn't feel shy and she wouldn't feel modest when he took her dress off. When he touched her breasts or the place where she was most needy, between her thighs. All she'd been conscious of was how intense the sensations were, how incredible it felt when he touched her. When that piercing blue gaze raked over her. And it wasn't cold any more, but blazing hot, electric.

And it was she who'd done that to him. It was she who'd melted the ice. No one special, no one all that different. Just a girl nobody had wanted.

But he wanted her. This king.

Except she couldn't see the icy, controlled king any more. The man above her was hungry and powerful, and as predatory as the lion he wore on his back. A man who had that intense, laser focus centred only on one thing—her.

There was more, of course there was more. And when he came to his knees between her thighs and pulled off her knickers, all she felt was relief. Because the need inside her was building again. He'd quenched it before, with his magic hands and his hot mouth, but just looking at him, just imagining what was going to happen, had the breath catching in her throat and desire sharpening between her thighs.

But not only her own pleasure. She was hungry to touch him too. Hungry to give him the same pleasure he was giving her, to share with him what she was feeling.

He was so cold. A mountain made of ice and stone, towering over the rest of the world. Powerful and remote, and very dangerous. Yet alone. She could sense that in him, because it was that loneliness that lay at the heart of her too. Whether he knew it or not, whether he was even aware of it, he felt it, because the evidence was there in the hunger in his eyes. As if he recognised the heat inside of her and wanted it for himself.

A mountain was lonely. A mountain was on its own.

She stared up at him as he looked down at her, his hungry gaze following the line of her naked body, zeroing in between her thighs.

Did he have anyone to keep him company? Did he have anyone at all who wanted to climb to the peak and sit beside him in the cold? Or was he a peak too dangerous to scale? There were avalanches and storms, fissures and crevasses. You could get hurt so very easily climbing a peak like that one and maybe that was how he liked it. Maybe he didn't want anyone near. Maybe he was happy being remote.

Her heart squeezed unexpectedly tight at the thought. No, it wasn't true. It wasn't. She would see that there was heat at the heart of him, there was passion and fire, and it was easy enough to spot now.

His eyes blazed as he got rid of his shirt and his hands dropped to the buckle of his belt, undoing it and pulling it off. His movements were slow, deliberate, but his jaw was tight. Tension rolled off him.

He was holding himself back, keeping that fire contained. And perhaps it was a tease for them both, or perhaps he didn't want to hurt her, because it was her first time after all.

But she didn't need him to. She was different now because he'd changed her. He'd turned her into someone else; she wasn't a nun any more. She was the woman who was going to set the fire inside him free.

Anna sat up, running her hands up his powerful thighs as he knelt there, watching him as he undid the fastenings of his trousers.

'Do you like what you see, little nun?' His voice was so deep, so dark. Like the sound of a glacier moving. Except this glacier wasn't cold any more. 'Do you want to touch me?'

'Yes.' She slid her hands over his hips, feeling the smoothness and heat of his bare skin, tracing the hard, chiselled lines of his stomach. 'Yes, so much.' And she did. She loved how powerful and strong he was. Loved how hot his skin was and how hard he felt under her palms.

Yes, he was a mountain. And she wanted to climb him.

Not that he gave her any opportunity.

Quickly, he divested himself of the rest of his clothes—far too quickly for her liking—but he didn't listen to her protests, gave her no time to look at him. One minute he was there with his trousers on, the next she was being pushed back on the couch cushions and he was over her again, and this time he was naked.

And he was glorious. A powerful machine of muscle and bone overlain with taut, velvety olive skin. He held himself above her, his biceps flexing with apparently no effort, and his strength excited her for reasons she couldn't explain.

She lifted her hands, ran her fingertips over him, stroking him, watching the piercing blue of his eyes get hotter. Then she glanced down and her breath caught.

He was long and thick, and when he noticed her look, he grabbed one of her hands and pushed it down between them, curling her fingers around him.

Anna gave a little gasp of delight. She'd had no idea that the most masculine part of a man would feel so smooth, like velvet. Or so hot. She'd had no idea he'd feel so hard either—not that she'd ever thought about it. Maybe if she had, she might have been more interested in sex. Certainly, if she'd known he'd feel like this she would have been.

Then again, the thought of touching any other man so intimately didn't have the same effect, so maybe it was just Adonis she wanted to touch.

'You look concerned,' he murmured roughly. 'Are you nervous?'

'No,' she said with absolute truth. 'I was just amazed at how good you feel.' She studied him, watching the lines of his face tighten as she squeezed him experimentally. 'Does that hurt? Or do you like me doing that?'

'No, it doesn't hurt. And yes, I like you doing that.'

'Oh. In that case—'

But he didn't let her finish, giving her a long, hard kiss, before pulling back again. She opened her mouth to protest, but then from somewhere he produced a silver packet and ripped it open. Contraception, she realised. He dealt with it then stretched himself over her, lazy as the lion he was.

'Now, then,' he said, his voice thick with sensual heat. 'Where were we? Ah, yes…' His hips shifted between her thighs, the head of his sex nudging at hers. Then he slid his hands beneath her, cupping her bottom, tilting her. His gaze held hers, level and intense. 'Are you ready for me, Anna?'

'Yes.' Excitement crowded in her throat, so intense she could barely force the word out.

He didn't wait. As soon as the word had left her lips, his hips flexed and he was pushing into her, a deep, slow thrust that tore another gasp from her throat. But it wasn't painful. No, strangely, despite what she'd heard, there was no pain at all. A vague kind of pull but then nothing but the feeling of her flesh parting for him, stretching around him. And it didn't feel like an invasion so much as a welcoming.

As if she was welcoming him home.

She trembled slightly at the immensity of the feeling that was spreading out through her chest. Of having him so close, inside her, part of her. It made her feel honoured, in a strange way, that he would allow this kind of intimacy.

Especially when you're not worthy of it.

Tears pricked at her eyes, and he stopped, deep inside her, looking down at her. 'Did I hurt you?' His voice sounded raw. 'Upset you?'

She shook her head, for the moment unable to speak, because the strange feeling had closed her throat. Clearly, from the way he was looking at her, this kind of reaction wasn't expected and it made her feel vulnerable in a way she hadn't when he'd first undressed her and touched her.

She didn't understand the feeling, so she reached up to him, took his face between her hands and drew his mouth down on hers, kissing him instead.

And then everything became a whole lot hotter and more desperate.

He began to move inside her, slow, deep thrusts that took hold of her desire and turned it sharper, a bright and intense pleasure moving through her.

She forgot her vulnerability. Forgot about worthiness or deserving. There was only him and the exquisite movement of his hips, the raw heat in his blue eyes, and the deep sounds of masculine pleasure that came from him every time he thrust.

It was amazing. She could barely stand it.

Anna wound her legs around his lean hips, following the rhythm he showed her, taking it and making it her own, lost to the intensity of the pleasure that gripped her.

And when the orgasm came, swelling inside her like a wave, she could only lie there staring up at him as it swept her up and drowned her in pleasure, making her cry his name aloud, holding onto him as if he were her anchor.

She was hardly aware of him moving faster, harder, his breathing as wild and as raw as hers, calling her name in answer, as he turned his face into her neck, and followed her into the tide.

Adonis tried to catch his breath and failed. The orgasm had felt like a cataclysm moving through him, a force of nature he couldn't control. It had broken over his head like a thunderstorm and all he'd been able to do was lie there with his head turned against Anna's skin, inhaling the scent of female arousal, lavender and sex, as pleasure blasted his world apart.

He couldn't move and so he didn't, shifting only so he wasn't lying directly on top of her because she was small and he didn't want to crush her.

Her own breathing was loud in his ear, a frantic, rushing sound that eventually slowed, the shaking in her body ebbing as the aftershocks faded, the hold she had on his shoulders loosening.

He felt raw and possessive and a little savage, none of which he should be feeling, and he found he'd pulled himself up to look at her, to see whether she was as wrecked as he was.

Her skin had gone a deep pink, curls of hair

sticking to her forehead, the sheen of perspiration on her brow and in the hollow of her throat. Her eyes were very dark, her mouth full and red and swollen from his kisses.

Yes, he'd wrecked her. He'd wrecked her utterly.

The savage possessiveness gripped him tighter, along with a fierce satisfaction that absolutely should not have been there.

You cannot let her get to you. Look what she made you do!

His gut lurched, a cold sensation gripping him.

He'd known taking her was wrong and yet he'd done it anyway. All because she'd touched him…all because she'd looked at him with silver burning in her eyes. And he could tell himself all kinds of lies about why he'd changed his mind, but the fact remained that he'd taken her because his control had slipped.

After all these years does your brother's pain still mean nothing?

Her hand came up and touched his mouth, a leisurely, sensual touch, and she smiled one of her luminous smiles. And he could feel something inside him respond, embers in the dead hearth of his heart glowing.

He moved instinctively, pulling away from her, pushing himself off her and up, beginning to reach for his clothes. The cold sensation was spreading through his blood now, icing the warmth she'd given him.

Because it wasn't true. He hadn't forgotten his brother's pain—the pain their father had put Xerxes through in order to teach Adonis what it truly meant to be a king. How emotion could be a weapon that in the wrong hands could take down a nation.

It had taken Adonis years to learn to get rid of those weaknesses in himself, to tame his own rebellious heart, and his failure to do so earlier had caused his little brother even more hurt. But those lessons had sunk in eventually and he couldn't forget them now. Couldn't throw all those lessons aside just because he wasn't able to resist one sexy little nun.

'Adonis?' Her voice, husky and soft, came from behind him. 'What's wrong?'

'Nothing.' He began to pull his clothes on, ruthlessly crushing the cold sensation in the pit of his stomach.

You put yourself first. That's what you always do.

'I think there's something,' she said. 'Did I do something wrong? Is that the—'

'No,' he interrupted flatly, making his voice hard. 'It isn't you.' He pulled his shirt on and turned around.

She was sitting on the couch, still naked, still pink. Her hair flowed over her shoulders in a pale gold tangle and she looked like any red-blooded man's wet dream, all lush female curves and touchable silky skin. A frown creased her brow and there was a concerned expression in her eyes, though whether that was for herself or for him, he wasn't sure.

'Then what is it?' she asked.

'Other things.' He knew he sounded dismissive, yet made no effort to temper his tone. The best thing for both of them right now was for her to leave. He'd made a mistake, but not one he'd compound by spending any more time with her than he had to.

His detachment might not be as perfect as he'd first thought, but he could fix that. Feeling possessive over one little nun wouldn't break him. He'd patch up his weaknesses, shore up his defences. No one would be able to use his emotions against him, because he simply wouldn't have any.

'Once that crown is on your head you as a person cease to exist,' Xenophon had told him once. *'You're not a brother. Not a son. Not a friend. You* are *Axios. Remember that. You are the king and there is no room for you to have or to be anything else.'*

He wasn't anything else. Once, he had been. But he wasn't now and he couldn't forget that.

'Do you need help finding your way back to your room?' he asked expressionlessly.

Disappointment flickered over her face. 'Adonis,' she began.

But the sound of his name made that tight sensation grip him again and he knew he couldn't allow her to use it. 'You may address me as sire.'

A spark of silver gleamed in her eyes.

You're hurting her.

It shouldn't matter. She had to be merely a woman with whom he'd spent a pleasant half-hour, nothing more. He couldn't afford for her to be anything else. His detachment was every-thing and right now she compromised it.

Still, she *was* his godmother's charge and he owed her more than a cold dismissal.

Gritting his teeth, he forced himself over to where she sat and crouched down in front of her. Not a good move when that brought him close to her naked body and he could feel the pull of desire rising inside him again, making him hard. Making him want to push her back down onto the cushions and teach her a few more new things.

But he only reached out and took her hands in his, holding them. 'We only had this moment,' he said, consciously keeping his voice gentle. 'I did tell you that.'

She stared at him a moment and then pulled her fingers from his. 'Yes, thank you, I know that,' she said coolly. 'There's no need to treat me like a child.'

He narrowed his gaze. 'Then don't look at me like one.'

'I'm not looking at you like anything.' She rose to her feet and moved past him, enveloping him in a wave of lavender, musk and sex, making him inexplicably want to reach out and grab her, to put his hands all over that beautiful body.

But he was strong and so he didn't. He rose to his feet too and watched her as she went to grab her clothes, beginning to pull them on in a series of small, deliberate movements.

That was a mistake.

Yes, obviously.

'You looked disappointed,' he said, again not sure why he was bothering to explain himself.

'You said nothing was wrong and that's clearly a lie.' She smoothed her dress. 'I was only disappointed you didn't want to share what it was with me.'

'I don't have to tell you. I'm not your boyfriend, Anna.'

She opened her mouth, probably to say something sharp. But then she must have thought better of it, because she closed it again, bending to pick up the tie for her hair instead. 'Yes,' she said in that cool voice, as she tied back her hair 'I'm well aware of that.'

'Anna—'

'You got up suddenly and all I wanted to know was whether there was anything bothering you. I wasn't asking you for a rundown of your entire life up to this point or for you to get down on your knees and declare your undying love. I only asked because it seemed like something was wrong, but if you didn't want to answer, you could have just said. You didn't need to treat me like some fragile flower who doesn't know the difference between casual sex and true love.'

His jaw tightened. This was not how he'd thought this would end.

How did you think it would end?

The question annoyed him. The whole situation annoyed him. Her feelings shouldn't touch him yet they had and he didn't know why.

He couldn't even tell himself that it wasn't his fault. Not when it was his control that had slipped. What was he thinking? He was normally much better at handling the women he slept with.

The women you sleep with are not normally nuns.

As if he needed yet another reminder of how he'd forgotten his father's lessons and allowed himself to think that he was a man.

He wasn't. He was a king.

Adonis remembered his crown and straightened. 'Then let us be very clear. That was casual sex. And there will not be another instance. We will go on as if it never happened.'

Her pretty grey eyes were snapping with temper and he thought he detected another flash of hurt. But then it was gone. 'Yes, fine.'

'You are simply my daughter's companion and that is all.'

'Of course, Your Majesty,' she said, and there was an edge to the words, a sarcasm that hadn't been there before. 'We wouldn't want it any other way.'

Your Majesty... You don't want her to call you that.

He ignored the thought, and shoved it hard from his head. 'Then you are dismissed,' he said coldly.

He thought she might argue with him further, but she didn't. She said nothing, simply turning on her heel and walking out.

And he tried to tell himself he wasn't disappointed about that. Not at all.

CHAPTER SEVEN

ANNA SPENT THE following couple of days furious and trying very hard not to be. The nuns had always cautioned against allowing negative emotions such as anger or jealousy to rule her and she'd thought she'd managed to overcome those weaknesses in herself.

But every time she thought of that moment in Adonis's—no, *the king's*—office, where he'd suddenly turned from a passionate man back into the cold, emotionless king, it made her so angry she could hardly stand it.

She might have been a virgin, but she wasn't stupid. And she might be sheltered, but she knew good sex didn't equal love. Even exceptional sex, though she had nothing to compare it to and, for all she knew, sex was like that for everyone every time.

So, she'd felt close to him. So, she'd wanted to know him. So, he'd made her feel things about herself that no one had ever made her feel before. So what?

Those were all feelings that had been prompted by physical pleasure, that was all.

She hadn't fallen magically in love with him. In fact, right now, she didn't even like him.

She tried to do what he'd told her, which was to forget all about what had happened between them and concentrate on Ione instead. But she found that at odd times she'd suddenly find herself remembering his hands on her skin, or the way he'd felt inside her; the pleasure that had bloomed throughout her entire body; the look in his blue eyes and the way her chest had tightened in wonder; the strange sadness that had gripped her as she'd thought about him being a mountain and having no one.

And something whispered to her that there was a reason she'd been so angry with him and so offended in the aftermath. A reason she hadn't protested at his cold dismissal.

It was because she was disappointed—worse, she was hurt. And even worse than that, she knew she had no reason to be. He'd been clear about what the sex would be between them. It was she who hadn't understood how it would affect her.

You were wrong. You are *a fragile flower.*

But she didn't want to think about that, so she didn't. Instead, she pursued her determination to help Ione. Adonis—*the king*—had sent word that her evening reports on Ione's progress would now be given to one of his aides rather than to himself, and he refused all requests for an audience as he was very busy at present.

It was enough to make her think that he was avoiding her, though she couldn't imagine why. Had it been that the passion between them had touched something in him, too? And now he couldn't be around her? But then, why would that be?

Whatever he was doing, it irritated her. So she went to Prince Xerxes instead, laying out her reasons for wanting to take Ione into Itheus without her usual contingent of soldiers.

Xerxes was—unlike his brother—understanding. He was also charming and so ridiculously handsome that he made Anna feel a little like a starstruck teenager. It turned out he had the same fears that Ione wasn't getting the attention she deserved either—he'd become a father six months earlier himself—and promised he'd take the matter to his brother personally.

He must have been far more persuasive than Anna because the next day Anna was granted permission to take Ione into the city with a contingent of two of the palace's most elite soldiers in plain clothes.

The day was beautiful, warm, and sunny, and Anna held fast to the little girl's hand as Ione charged around Itheus's narrow cobbled streets, loudly telling Anna about this thing or that thing. *That's the church where Uncle Xerxes married Aunt Calista. That's where Papa married Mama.*

That caused a small pang of grief in Anna's heart. Ione didn't seem to mind talking about her mother. And after they visited the shop that was renowned throughout Axios, even throughout Europe, for its ice cream, and came outside into the bustling streets, licking melting ice cream from the crisp waffle cones, Anna asked another couple of questions about her.

Ione said very matter-of-factly that something had been wrong with Mama's heart and so she'd died when Ione was still a baby. Was that a playground? Could they go over and play in it?

That the little girl couldn't remember her mother made Anna's heart ache in sympathy. The princess was so very alone. Her father was cold, kept his daughter at a distance, and so she was left to an army of people who looked after her and cared for her. But they wouldn't love her as a mother would. They wouldn't want to get to know her, chat to her, treat her as though she was an ordinary, albeit very special, little girl, and not the heir to the throne.

Resolve settled down through Anna as she wiped the ice cream from Ione's face then let her go and play in the playground. The Reverend Mother had been right to send her to Axios, regardless of whether the old lady thought she was sending Anna to the king or not. Anna wasn't here for him. She was here for this lonely, motherless girl. And she was uniquely qualified to understand Ione, because she'd been a lonely, motherless girl herself. The nuns had given her a home and they'd given her love, but it wasn't a mother's love. It wasn't warm or personal. It was distant and stern and vaguely disapproving.

Like the king.

Anna watched Ione squealing with laughter as she and another girl raced around the playground, the two guards loitering at a discreet distance, and determination settled in her heart.

This little girl needed more than that. She was passionate and giving, with a bright, sparky spirit. And though she might be motherless, she wasn't fatherless. She still had a parent. That was who she needed, not a large contingent of guards and nannies. Not even a stranger like herself to 'manage' her behaviour.

No, she needed her father.

Does he even know how to be one?

Emotion coiled inside her, bittersweet and raw, because she suspected she knew the answer to that. Adonis was a mountain and mountains were distant and icy. They protected and yet they sat apart. They did not bother themselves with the people who lived at their base.

Anna turned away from the children playing and glanced behind her, at the mountains, the ones that reached high above Itheus, all rocky crags and sharp edges. She looked at the palace that had been built into the side of them, as sharp and as dark as the king who ruled it. A medieval fortress, closely guarded and well defended.

Like his heart.

Did he even have one? Well, if he did, he needed to open it. For his daughter's sake. And there probably wasn't another person in the entire world who would dare demand that he do it. No one but Anna.

Prince Xerxes had his own daughter to look after and the army of servants and guards would never dare challenge the king. But Anna would.

And if it gets you sent home in disgrace?

Then at least she would have tried. Nothing would change if she didn't try.

The day was such a success that the king relented and allowed Anna to take Ione to the playground a number of times in the days following, and even to the swimming pool in Itheus, rather than the palace's own pool. But he still refused all requests for Anna to speak to him directly. He was always in meetings or away from the palace, or undertaking public duties or some other thing that meant she couldn't talk to him.

Even after her 'probation period' of two weeks was up, and nothing further was said about her returning home to England, Anna wasn't granted a personal audience.

So, yes, he *was* avoiding her. Which was ridiculous, not to mention puzzling. Because why would he? Sure, they'd had sex, but he'd told her to pretend it had never happened and that was exactly what she was doing. Could he not do the same? Or was he genuinely busy?

Either way, it annoyed her. She wasn't sure how long she would be kept on here, and, although Ione seemed to be less disruptive whenever Anna was around, she was still prone to inappropriate tantrums and reckless behaviour. And Anna thought that wasn't going to get any better until His Royal Majesty deigned to spend more time with his daughter, though where that would leave Anna herself, she wasn't sure.

One thing she was sure of: Ione had come to trust her and she wasn't going to let the little girl down by not at least making an attempt to talk to the king.

No one else could do this. Only her. And it

mattered because she didn't want to see Ione grow up as she had, in the company of distant people who cared for her, but only in a detached way. Who only saw her as a collection of behaviours that needed managing, a future monarch in Ione's case, and not as an actual person.

However, it wasn't until nearly four weeks after she'd first taken Ione to the playground that Anna eventually spotted her opportunity.

The king was giving a special function for dignitaries from various European countries and, since it would be the first time he wouldn't be closeted away and guarded assiduously, she'd have the perfect opportunity to approach him. He could hardly send her away or drag her from the room in front of all his assembled guests—not that she'd interrupt him and demand he speak to her while he was talking to others, of course. She'd somehow get herself into the ball, even though she wouldn't be invited, and then wait for an opportunity. And there would be one, she was certain of it.

Over the past few weeks she'd amassed a few items of clothing, purchased from the salary the king paid her, but a ballgown wasn't one of those things. However, Princess Calista came to her aid, finding her a dress to borrow for the night from one of Axios's most talented designers, while offering her stylist's services to do her hair and make-up. Anna decided not to lie about the reasons for slipping into the ball even though she hadn't been invited, and Calista had been wholeheartedly on Anna and Ione's side.

And so, a week later, Anna found herself standing in front of a small side door—a staff entrance—that led into the grand ballroom of the palace, dressed in a stunning ballgown of ice-blue silk and silver lace, with an overskirt of silver net sewn with crystals, with her hair, golden and gleaming, piled high on her head and perfect make-up, ready to crash the king's reception.

She felt strange, utterly unlike herself, as if she'd put on someone else's clothing. Nerves fluttered in her stomach, making her feel slightly sick. She'd been feeling off-colour the past couple of days, though it hadn't turned into anything more than tiredness and the occasional bout of nausea, so she'd mostly ignored it. Right now, though, it felt worse, making it difficult to find the calm that usually got her through the most trying days in the convent.

This was a move the Reverend Mother wouldn't approve of, that was certain, but then, Anna wasn't doing this for herself, just so she could go to a party and wear a ballgown. Or even to see the king she couldn't stop thinking about.

She was doing this for Ione.

The staff member leaned forward and pushed open the door, and abruptly Anna was thrust into a massive room full of beautiful people wearing beautiful clothes, where the air buzzed with the sound of conversation and the tones of a small orchestra played in one corner.

The vaulted stone ceiling was crisscrossed with heavy beams around which coiled lots of delicate lights. The stone walls had been softened by the inevitable tapestries, along with silken wall hangings. Pots of trees had been placed everywhere as well as enormous tubs of flowers. There were even fountains, giving the illusion of a lovely and elaborate garden that had been brought inside.

It was beautiful, and for a second Anna wanted to simply enjoy it for herself.

But that wasn't why she was here.

Steeling herself, she stepped forward into the crowd.

Adonis stood next to the wall beside one of the big potted rhododendrons, taking advantage of a minute's gap in the constant round of small talk to scan the crowd, to make sure the evening was proceeding as planned.

The celebration to mark the signing of Axios's latest treaty wasn't something he was particularly enjoying. Unlike his brother, who loved a good party, Adonis did *not* like parties. Nevertheless, many Axians did like to have a fuss made, so he'd ensured the maximum amount of fuss for this particular occasion, opening the royal wine cellars and making sure the royal chefs did not disappoint for the official dinner.

And, indeed, they had not.

A triumph, people were saying, which he took as Axios's due. He might not like parties, but even he could appreciate how a good one could earn respect.

The crowd in the ballroom shifted and turned, the air full of conversation and the sounds of the orchestra. Jewels and sequins sparkled, the light also glinting off medals and cufflinks, while people laughed and talked and drank vintage champagne from the best palace crystal.

Restlessness coiled inside him. A familiar restlessness. It had been rattling around and around inside him like a lion pacing before the bars of his cage, and nothing seemed to get rid of it. He'd been spending long hours in his gym and in the pool, working himself into physical exhaustion, but that hadn't helped. Even rounds in the boxing ring hadn't got rid of it.

He'd tried to fill his days as much as he could with the endless demands of kingship, trying to ignore it, but that hadn't helped either. At the end of each day he lay awake in his bed, that restlessness eating away inside him, and he'd have to get up and walk the corridors just to satisfy it.

As a consequence, he was in a foul mood.

It didn't help that a part of him knew exactly why he was restless, but it was a part he didn't want to acknowledge and so he didn't. Except during the day, when sometimes he could hear the sounds of his daughter's laughter, and along with it the sound of another laugh. Deeper and a little huskier than Ione's clear bell tones, with a warmth that crept through him, touching something inside him. And it made his heart race and his body harden.

And when he walked the palace corridors at night, he sometimes caught the vague scent of lavender and sweetness, and that had the same effect, making desire wrap itself around him, choking him.

Xerxes unfortunately noticed his temper and had asked him what was wrong, but Adonis had ignored him. He didn't want to talk about the real reason he couldn't settle, because it shouldn't have been a problem.

And he didn't know why it was.

You do.

Adonis ignored that thought completely, concentrating his attention on the crowd. He would soon have to resume his tour of the ballroom, talking to all the necessary people...

A glitter caught his eye, his attention drawn to the progress of a woman wending her way through the crowd. The gown she wore was silvery blue and looked as if the voluminous skirts had been scattered all over with tiny diamonds or raindrops, catching the light as she moved. It was strapless, the bodice cupping a pair of the most perfect breasts he'd ever seen and hugging curvaceous hips. Her bare shoulders glowed like pale satin in the light, her blonde hair piled on her head in delicate curls like a fall of winter sunlight. Her face was heart-shaped and delectable, with a mouth made for sin, and she was beautiful, glowing.

His body hardened instantly.

Perhaps after this ridiculous party was over he could make her acquaintance, because the one thing he hadn't tried to stem this restlessness was sex. He hadn't had a woman since Anna. He'd told himself he'd been too busy, that he'd indulge himself later, but later hadn't come so far. He'd found himself…unenthusiastic about the idea of someone else. Yet not now. He watched her come through the crowd, realising with a start that she was making her way very determinedly towards him, and she was familiar in some way. She reminded him of his little nun with her hair and her skin, and those beautiful curves…

Realisation hit him like a lightning strike.

It *was* his little nun, looking like a princess and coming towards him in that single-minded way she had. How he hadn't known her instantly he couldn't fathom, because there was no mistaking those misty grey eyes or the stubborn slant of her chin.

He stared, drinking in the sight of her. It felt like weeks since he'd seen her—it *had* been weeks since he'd seen her—and he hadn't realised how hungry he was for the sight of her until now.

It was wrong, of course, but he couldn't drag his gaze away.

What was she doing here? He hadn't invited her. This wasn't the kind of event she should be attending. And yet here she was, making straight for him, dressed in a magnificent gown with her hair and make-up perfect... If he hadn't noticed that her hands were clasped tightly in front of her and that even under the make-up she was slightly pale, he would have said she belonged here. The most beautiful jewel in the crown.

His guards loitering a discreet distance away instantly came to attention as she approached, but he shook his head slightly and they relaxed again. He could have had them usher her from the room before she even reached him, but it was clear she was determined to talk to him and he couldn't think of a reason why she shouldn't.

You've thought of plenty of reasons for weeks.

It was true he'd refused all her requests for a meeting, but that was because he'd been extremely busy. And yes, he'd delegated her nightly reports on Ione's progress to an assistant, but again, he'd been extremely busy. It had nothing to do with how she threatened his detachment. Nothing at all.

However, it had been weeks since he'd seen her and surely he was master of himself enough that meeting her wouldn't be a problem. He could spare her a couple of minutes.

Yet his heart beat strangely fast as she approached, his body was hard, and the man who was somehow still alive inside him, the man who should have been displaced entirely by the king, wanted to take her in his arms and find somewhere quiet, somewhere dark, and resume what they'd started in his office weeks ago.

But that could not happen, not again. Nothing had changed.

He was still a king and distance was still required. He would not take her again, no matter what the man inside him wanted.

So he watched her approach, remaining unmoving. People would be looking at him because a king was always under scrutiny, but, since he was relatively hidden by the rhododendrons, he wouldn't be visible to that many people. And neither would she.

'Your Majesty,' she said formally, coming to a stop in front of him and sweeping into a low and graceful curtsey. 'Do you have a moment?'

He eyed her. It really was a magnificent gown, the light glittering off the crystals sewn into her skirts. Where had she got it?

'I do not recall inviting you to this party, Anna.' He kept his tone flat. 'And yet here you are, in a couture gown, with your hair and make-up done...'

She rose from her curtsey, her colour high, her eyes glittering silver, much like her gown. 'No, I know I wasn't invited. Princess Calista helped me with the gown and her stylist did my make-up and hair. I wasn't going to turn up at something like this wearing my grey dress, if that's what you were wondering.'

'What I was wondering was why you are here at all. Especially when, as I said, I did not invite you.'

She gave him a narrow look, her hands clasped tightly in front of her. 'Since you refused all requests for a meeting, I had to find some way of talking to you directly. This seemed the perfect opportunity.'

She was enterprising, his little nun.

Yours?

Just a figure of speech. Of course she wasn't his.

'I've been busy,' he said shortly. 'What is this about?' He very much hoped it wasn't going to be about what had gone on in his office, yet what else could it be?

She was very cool and collected, but he could see the familiar little spark that spoke of her temper all the same, which meant he had to be careful. He found her bright sparks of emotion altogether too fascinating, though at least now he was aware of where his weaknesses lay.

'What do you think this is about?' She seemed annoyed that he didn't know.

'If you're here to talk about what happened in my office—'

'Of course I'm not here to talk about that,' she interrupted, apparently feeling that she could interrupt a king at will. 'I'm here to talk about Ione.'

Surprise rippled through him, closely followed by disappointment, which made no sense. He hadn't wanted to talk about what had happened between them, and Ione was far more of an important subject.

'What about her?' he asked. 'My assistant has been keeping me updated with her progress and I'm pleased with what you've been doing with her.' And he was. Ione had been doing very well by all accounts, though he hadn't seen much of an improvement in her behaviour the few times he'd glimpsed her.

Perhaps she's only good with other people.

It was a thought that did nothing for his own temper.

'She is doing well and has been enjoying the outings I take her on,' Anna said. 'And thank you for granting permission, by the way.'

Ah, yes. The outings. Xerxes had plagued him about that for hours, presenting argument after argument. But it hadn't been until Xerxes had mentioned his being too like their father for comfort that he'd changed his mind. Xenophon had been brutal, but Adonis wasn't, and so he'd given in.

'You can thank my brother for that,' he said coolly.

'And I did.' Anna gave him a stern look. 'But outings aside, Ione's behaviour probably won't get any better until she spends more time with her father.'

He stiffened at the inescapable hint of judgment in her tone. 'Are you questioning me?'

'Yes, actually, I am.' Anna took a step towards him. 'I know you're very busy, that being a king is time-consuming. But the truth is that she needs more of you, Adonis. And she doesn't get it.'

Heat lanced through him at her casual use of his name, as though she had a right to it. As though he was simply a man and she a woman, naked in his arms.

'I did not give you leave to use my name,' he said coldly, trying to lock down the anger at his own reaction to her. 'You forget yourself, Sister.'

But of course she wasn't cowed by him. She never had been. And instead of inclining her head and accepting her chastisement, she took another step, so she was right in front of him, determination and anger glowing bright in her eyes. 'I don't care. You might be a king, *sire,* but you're also a father. And your little girl needs you.'

She's right. And you know it too.

Hot anger and a smothering sense of guilt tore through him, though he tried to fight it. Because deep inside the heart he tried to tell himself he didn't have, he *did* know it.

But being a father would always come second to being a king, and Ione had to learn that. Because one day she would have to make the same choices that he had.

'Choose, Adonis,' his father had demanded, the day after Adonis had successfully rescued his brother from captivity in the desert, risking the entire succession of Axios to do so. *'I have told you again and again that you cannot be my heir and a brother at the same time, that there will always be an enemy who will use someone you love against you. So you must choose. Your brother or your throne? Which is it to be?'*

Of course he'd chosen the throne. Every time his father had made him choose, he'd always chosen the throne. And not for the power, but because that was his duty.

Ione would have to learn that too when she was old enough. He wouldn't teach her the way his own father had taught him, of course, but when it came time for her to become the Lioness of Axios, he would sit her down and explain why detachment in a monarch was important.

Are you so sure that's true? Do you really want her to turn into what you've become?

Adonis crushed the thought. He had become a king. What was so terrible about that?

'Ione is not more important than my subjects,' he snapped, some of the anger that gripped him leaking out in his voice no matter how hard he tried to stop it. 'I am responsible for millions—including at least a million children—so please forgive me if they take precedence over the needs of one already happy child.'

Anna's expression flickered, something entering her eyes that he didn't like the look of one bit. Her gaze narrowed and she took another step, her skirts brushing closer to him, and he was suddenly surrounded by the scent of musk and lavender, by the warmth of her. Making the breath catch in his throat.

'But she's not happy, Adonis,' she said quietly, her voice very level. 'And neither, I think, are you.'

Happy. What did he know about being happy? Happiness was just another useless emotion he couldn't allow himself to have.

And your daughter? You want that for her?

He ignored the thought. 'Happiness is irrelevant. Rulers do not need to be happy in order to rule.'

Anna's gaze searched his. 'No, but happiness is necessary for children, don't you think?'

'No,' he said before he could stop himself. 'My childhood was unhappy and I survived.'

Concern flickered over her face and she began to lift one of her hands, as if she'd been going to touch him before remembering where she was.

It was a good thing she stopped herself. Touching him would have been a bad idea.

'Oh?' There was concern in her voice now, too. 'What happened?'

And, looking into her steady grey eyes, he felt the strangest urge fill him, almost as if he wanted to tell her.

To tell her about how, when he was seven, he

and his mother had been carjacked on the way back to the palace from a function. How their enemies had been expecting the king to be riding with them and were disappointed, demanding to know where he was. And how his mother had refused to give away her husband's location and so they'd hurt her. And because he'd loved her and because he was desperate to save her, Adonis had told them what she wouldn't. She'd tried to grab one of their guns after that, to stop them, but they shot her.

About how his father's bodyguards had managed to hold off the resulting attack, though Xenophon had been injured. And how afterwards his father had told him that her death was his fault, that if Adonis had only been strong in the face of her pain, the palace guards might have been able to rescue them and her death might have been avoided.

'*Choose,*' his father had said after her funeral. '*You must choose, Adonis. The throne must come before everything. Even before your own mother. You can be my son or you can be my heir, but you cannot be both.*'

He had chosen the throne, of course he had. His younger brother had been too little to take over and Adonis had always been the responsible one. And once his mother had gone, he'd only had his father left.

Yes, he could tell her that.

Or he could tell her how Xenophon had been extra-vigilant after his mother had died, making it his mission to 'harden up' his oldest son. He'd given Adonis a puppy and then, when the dog had grown, had given Adonis a gun and told him to kill it.

Adonis hadn't been able to. He'd been twelve and furious, weeping with rage at himself and his inability to do what his father had asked and shoot his beloved pet. He'd tried, but his heart had got in the way. Again, he'd been weak. In the end he'd had to give the dog to someone else—his father would only have killed the animal himself if Adonis hadn't got rid of it—and hoped that that would be enough for his father.

It wasn't enough. Xenophon had punished him, told him that the lessons in detachment would continue until Adonis learned how to put his feelings completely to the side, because their enemies would show no mercy and so neither could Xenophon.

Or he could tell her about how Xenophon

had kidnapped Xerxes, hiding his own identity to test Xerxes's strength and will, torturing him in a cell beneath the palace. He'd ensured that Adonis had been present behind a locked door, with instructions that he absolutely must not interfere. Adonis had had to sit there, listening to his brother's cries, knowing that the moment he tried to get to Xerxes, Xenophon would only redouble his efforts. The only way to end Xerxes's suffering was to do what his father wanted, to lock those feelings away, to endure.

So he had. He'd turned his heart into a block of ice, into stone. A dead hearth in which nothing burned. It had been hard, because his emotions had always been fierce, raw things and he'd found it difficult to contain them.

But he'd had to. For his mother's sake. For his brother's. For his country's.

Yes, he could tell her all those things. But he wouldn't. They weren't her burdens to bear; they were his.

'No,' he repeated, icily. 'I'm afraid that's none of your business, little nun.'

That expression was in her eyes again, the one that made his chest hurt. And it made him angry for no good reason. Her hand was rising again and he knew she'd forget herself this time, and that couldn't happen.

'Anna.' He kept his voice hard. 'Don't forget where we are.'

She took a small, audible breath, her half-lifted hand dropping again. But the expression in her eyes didn't change. 'I'm sorry.'

Her voice sounded small and he had the impression that she wasn't apologising for forgetting herself, but for something else. Something deeper. It made him want to ask what she meant, but already he'd stood here too long. Already he'd spent too much time with her, especially when he had dozens of other people he had to talk to before the night was out.

'Is that all?' he asked without inflection. 'Forgive me, I have many other commitments tonight.'

It was a dismissal and he made sure it sounded like one, and he could see a bolt of hurt dart through her eyes. He didn't like it, but there wasn't any other way to handle this. Besides, she was the one who'd cornered him, not the other way around.

He waited for her to curtsey and leave, but it

took her a moment to realise that was what he was expecting. Finally she did, and dutifully sank down. Yet as she was rising he caught the sudden drain of colour in her pretty pink cheeks. And he saw her sway. And when her hand came out as if to grab hold of something he was there.

And when she fell he caught her, holding her close as she fainted away in his arms.

CHAPTER EIGHT

ANNA CAME SLOWLY back to consciousness to the sound of a man talking quietly. He had a very deep voice that she found inexplicably soothing, and so she didn't open her eyes immediately. She was lying on something hard and yet incredibly warm, that deep, gravelly voice was all around her, and she didn't want to move. She felt safe and protected in a way she hadn't for years, if ever, and, since she was tired, more tired than she'd ever felt in her life, she saw no reason to open her eyes.

His voice continued and she drifted for a moment, content to be exactly where she was. Then he stopped talking and silence enveloped her. It was so warm and she was being held, and she didn't want to wake up, so she didn't, drifting back into unconsciousness for a little while longer.

When she came to again, strong arms were still around her, and she was still warm, though a fresh breeze was playing around her ankles and moving over her face. There was movement too, as if she was being carried somewhere. She didn't like it, so she turned her face into the hard warmth she was being held against, and determinedly kept her eyes closed.

Some more time passed, and then a very loud noise rattled through her head, and it sounded so much like a helicopter starting up that she cracked open her eyes just to check.

And then she blinked.

Because it was true. She was being held tightly in someone's lap and she was in a helicopter. A helicopter that was rising up into the night sky and soaring like a bird over the mountains, the lights of Itheus and the palace disappearing beneath it.

Itheus…the palace…

The king….

The breath rushed into her lungs, memory swamping her.

Of walking into the glittering crowds to find him, and then spotting him on his own at last, so tall and broad in black evening clothes, his position only given away by the aura of power that surrounded him. That and the discreet crowned lion fashioned in gold that was pinned to his lapel.

He'd let her approach, watching her with those icy blue eyes, and she could feel something intense and strong pull inside her, something she'd been ignoring for weeks. And she'd known in that instant that it wasn't just for Ione's sake that she'd been trying to get a meeting with him. It was for herself as well.

Because it wasn't until he was right in front of her, the sheer magnetism of his presence drawing her, tugging at her, that she'd realised how much she'd been longing to see him again. Just once. Just to be near him.

That longing had gripped her so hard she'd had to clasp her hands together to stop them from reaching for him. And it had taken everything she had not to ask him for another night. Or even five minutes and only to talk. But she had her pride and he'd been very clear, and besides, it was Ione that mattered, not herself.

But it had been obvious that he neither wanted her, nor had the time to give his daughter.

'Happiness is irrelevant. A ruler doesn't need to be happy in order to rule...'

He'd said that before mentioning his own unhappy childhood, and her heart had twisted. And, given that bleak statement, she might have called her mission a failure.

Yet when she'd asked him to tell her about what had made that childhood so unhappy, she'd had the impression that he'd wanted to. Something had flickered deep in his eyes, a momentary glimpse of something more human. Something that had looked like pain.

And that sense had assailed her once again, of his isolation. His loneliness. The mountain who had no one.

It had made her heart twist in helpless sympathy.

And she'd been desperate to know more. But then he'd dismissed her and the nausea she'd been fighting all day had turned over inside her and blackness had crawled along the edges of her vision. And then…nothing.

Until she'd come to in someone's arms.

You know whose arms.

She moved, her heartbeat racing, but a warm hand rested lightly on her head and a deep rumble of sound vibrated against her ear. The noise of the rotors prevented her from hearing what it was that he said, but his touch calmed her almost instantly.

Of course it was him. His distinctive scent was around her, his heat soaking through the material of her gown, the steady, strong beat of his heart against her ear.

She had no idea where she was going or why, but somehow that didn't matter. And she wasn't afraid. The king might be ice-cold, but he'd never hurt her.

Anna relaxed against him and closed her eyes. She didn't sleep, only let herself enjoy this endless moment, with the noise of the helicopter flying through the night somewhere mysterious, held in the strong arms of a king.

But it ended far too soon.

Anna's eyes opened as the helicopter landed, the rotors slowing, and then cold air was washing around her, bringing the scent of the sea, and she was being carried in darkness along a lighted path.

'I can walk,' she protested, her voice sounding husky. She could hear waves crashing against a distant shore and smell salt in the air.

'No,' the king said. And, since there was no loosening of his hold on her and because she was actually quite happy where she was, she didn't fight him.

She did allow herself to look up though. The lights of the path illuminated his harsh, handsome features. They were set in hard lines, brutal as stone and just as unyielding, and she felt, for the first time, a little quiver of fear.

Whatever had happened and wherever they were, it was because of something serious.

Yet his hold was gentle, and he carried her effortlessly, and, even though there was that fear there, she kept herself relaxed.

The path wound its way through a rocky garden to a small house constructed of white stone with lots of windows. It was lit with hidden lighting, making the place glow like alabaster, warm and inviting.

So. Definitely not a prison, then. Not that she'd done anything wrong, but being transported in the dead of night was always a worry.

A woman opened the double front doors as they approached, potted olive trees standing on either side, and then they were in a pretty tiled entranceway with plain whitewashed walls.

The king said something Anna didn't catch to the woman and then she stepped outside, shutting the doors behind her. Anna found herself carried down a short, wide hallway and through into a lounge area.

Again, the floor was tiled, the walls whitewashed. Big windows faced the darkness, while luxurious low couches and chairs carved from heavy dark wood and covered in plain white linen were arranged around them. Thick cushions in jewel tones brought colour to the room, while on the floor was a cheerful rag-rolled rug in what looked like bright silks. The king walked to the couch and gently deposited her on it, but he didn't sit. He only stood there, looking down at her, tall and forbidding in his black evening clothes, the golden lion pin gleaming on his breast.

'I suppose you're wondering why you're here,' he said at last. 'Anna, why didn't you tell me you were pregnant?'

Anna blinked, not understanding. 'Excuse me?'

'You fainted in my arms. I had my own personal doctor attend you and he was able to run a number of blood tests. This included a pregnancy test to eliminate the possibility.' The king's face remained hard as granite. 'It was not eliminated and is no longer a possibility. It is a reality.'

She opened her mouth but nothing came out. A cold feeling moved through her, starting at her extremities, making her fingers and toes go numb. Shock. But then, she could only be shocked if it was true, surely. And it couldn't be true. This was all a terrible joke that he was playing on her...

But his hard expression didn't change and his beautiful mouth looked as far from smiling as it ever had.

It's not a joke.

The tiredness that had been dogging her, the nausea that had come and gone, making her feel so awful...

Her lips were now numb and she couldn't feel her hands either, or her feet. 'But we used protection,' she said faintly.

'Protection that apparently failed.' His gaze was so sharp it felt as if it could cut. 'You didn't know?'

Anna shook her head. The possibility had never occurred to her, not once. And now... 'I can't be.' Her voice sounded strange and distant. 'My vows... Oh...' Her heart was beating far too fast and she couldn't breathe. All she could think about was the Reverend Mother and what she'd say, and this last, perhaps greatest mistake. There would be no place in the convent for her now…

Helpless tears filled her eyes, loss gripping her. The convent had been the only home she'd ever known, the nuns the only people who'd ever wanted her, and she'd tried so hard to be good. To be the kind of nun they wanted her to be. But there was no hope of that now.

Pull yourself together. This isn't about you.

Anna swallowed and found she'd put a hand on her stomach, as if to protect the tiny germ of life inside her from her own thoughts. And underneath the shock and the numbness was a small thread of wonder with strands of steely determination woven through it.

She'd been abandoned as a baby; her mother hadn't wanted her then and she hadn't wanted her years later, either. But Anna wouldn't make the same decisions her mother had. Her child would be wanted. Her child would be loved.

She looked up to find the king very close, having taken a couple of steps towards her, obviously to provide some support. But already the shock and self-pitying thoughts that had assailed her were fading away, crushed by the growing strength of her determination.

Anna pushed herself to her feet and met his blue gaze, watching in some satisfaction as surprise rippled across his roughly handsome features. 'I don't care what you say.' Her voice this time was heavy with certainty and almost as hard as his. 'I'm keeping this baby. And I will never get rid of it. This baby is mine.'

A deep blue glow sparked in his gaze. 'I haven't said anything, and if you think I'm going to order you to get rid of it, then you're sadly mistaken. This baby is mine also and of course you will be keeping it.'

Somewhere inside her something instinctive and old as time warmed in approval and satisfaction, but she ignored it. A wave of emotion was building in her, part shock, part anger, part joy and a few other things that she couldn't untangle. It made her heart race. The numbness had receded and so had the light-headedness and nausea, leaving behind it nothing but flames. She was on fire, burning up with reaction and nowhere to direct it.

Nowhere but at him.

'Are you sure about that?' she shot back heedlessly. 'When you don't have time for the child you already have?'

The blue spark in his eyes became a flame, joining the ones already burning inside her, the intense tangle of emotion coalescing into something much hotter and much more definite.

He was so close and his scent was around her, his big, hard body right in front of her. And she could feel the heat of him, the fire that burned inside of him despite his icy exterior. The same fire that burned inside of her, and suddenly she was hungry. It had been weeks since she'd touched him, weeks since she'd been anywhere near him, and it felt like too much. She was so lonely and here he was, his heat burning away the dark.

The baby wasn't real, not in this moment, and the future impossible to contemplate, but he was real and he was hot. He was strong and powerful, and he filled up her entire world.

She lifted her hands to touch him but he caught her wrists, his fingers like manacles of fire on her delicate skin, his strength overwhelming.

'Adonis.' His name came out, part prayer, part plea, part command.

And the blue flame in his eyes leapt high.

'Please,' she said.

His fingers tightened, and that was the only warning she got as he lowered his head and took her mouth.

There was no thought, only action. Only the fierceness of the anger he couldn't control, no matter how hard he tried, and it came thick and hot, leaping high as she challenged him, flinging a truth at him that he didn't want to hear. And then when her silver gaze had caught fire, that anger had exploded into a deep and instinctive desire.

He didn't know what had changed, whether it was simply their chemistry reacting in proximity to one another, needing only a spark to ignite it, weeks of denial turning into wildfire, or whether it was something deeper.

Something to do with her carrying his child and the decision he'd made as he held her in his arms on the flight through the darkness to his island, his mind already sorting through possibilities and plans after the doctor's shock revelation. He could have laid her on the seat next to him, but the strong sense of possessiveness that had gripped him on hearing the news, the same possessiveness he'd felt the night he'd first taken her, wouldn't leave him. This time he didn't resist it and kept hold of her instead.

He had been angry—no, more like furious—with himself. Because it was no one's fault but his that this had happened. He was the one with the experience and he was the one who knew that even with condoms there was a small failure rate. And there was nothing to be done about it. It had happened and the fierce protectiveness that had rushed through him, as strong as the possessiveness, wouldn't be denied, no matter what justifications he gave himself.

He knew what he must do. Nothing was certain until after the twelve-week mark and it was still early days, but that didn't matter. There was Ione to consider, and what Anna had said to him at the celebration, about how Ione wasn't happy, had stuck in his head.

Happiness was a feeling he didn't need, but, no matter his father's training, he found he couldn't bear the thought that his daughter didn't need it either. He knew what the expectations were of an heir and how heavily they had sat on his shoulders. How sometimes he'd wanted his parents to be normal parents, who put him first and not the crown. Yet they never had. Even in those last moments, his mother had been acting to protect her husband, not him.

He could do that for Ione, though. He could give her someone who would put her first. Someone loving and loyal, someone who could perhaps provide him with some physical relief too. A wife, in other words. He hadn't planned on marrying again, not wanting to put a potential partner through the misery Sophia had endured. But perhaps it would be different this time with Anna. He would set it out plainly for her, like a job. And she could also choose to view it that way if that was preferable to her.

She wasn't from an aristocratic family, but his kingship was secure. It didn't matter who he married, and Anna was the logical choice, even if her pregnancy didn't go ahead.

After all, it wasn't as if she loved him.

You thought that about Sophia. And Anna is passionate; she feels things deeply. You can't possibly expect her to remain unengaged.

But he refused that thought, just as he'd refused it as she'd flung her accusation about the lack of attention he gave the one child he already had. She'd stood straight and tall, blazing, not like a little nun, but like steel tempered in fire, becoming stronger and sharper.

He hadn't been able to stop himself as she'd spoken his name, the blaze in her eyes changing into passion as he felt his own desire rise. He didn't want to stop though. He'd been dreaming of her, of her mouth under his, of the sweet heat between her thighs and the soft curves of her breasts, for weeks, and he was hungry. So very, very hungry. And it was a sharp, raw thing that clawed at his insides with a deep, insistent ache.

He shouldn't give in to the intensity of his need and he knew it. He knew, too, that his detachment was already compromised from their previous encounter.

But he hadn't been able to resist.

She'd awoken the lion and this lion was ravenous.

His grip tightened on her wrists and, though she made an attempt to pull away, he didn't let her, pushing her wrists behind her back and holding them there. She groaned as her mouth opened beneath his and he tasted her, the hot sweetness of her like summer wine.

And just like that night in his office, there was no shyness in her and she held nothing back, her kiss that of a starving woman and he a feast brought before her.

She made an insistent, demanding sound, pushing herself against him, her soft curves pressed to his body, and his hunger sharpened further, gaining a possessive edge which was choking in its intensity.

He should have resisted that too, but he didn't. Because as her teeth sank into his lower lip, the lion escaped its cage entirely.

Adonis growled, gripping her wrists hard in one hand and jerking down the bodice of her gown with the other, baring her to the waist. Then he cupped one breast, squeezing gently, testing the weight of it. Her skin was silky and warm in his palm, and she gasped against his mouth, arching into him.

He kissed her harder, deeper, teasing her hard nipple with his thumb, then pinching it lightly. She shuddered, a low moan escaping her. Her soft curves were crushed against him, the heat of her skin burning through the black wool of his tuxedo, and suddenly the clothing separating them was too much.

He wanted her naked, wanted skin on skin with nothing between them.

She is yours now.

Yes, she was.

He let go of her straining wrists, found her zip and tugged it down. Then he peeled the gown away from her, leaving her naked but for her plain white knickers.

'Adonis,' she gasped, reaching for him, but he pushed her down onto the couch.

'Stay there,' he ordered harshly as she tried to get up, shrugging off his jacket and dropping it carelessly onto the floor.

She stilled, watching him, her breasts rising and falling fast and hard with her quickened breathing. She was a beautiful sight, all white skin and luscious curves and rosy nipples. Her pretty hair was still piled on top of her head, but he would take that down. He would ruin it. He would ruin her for anyone but him.

Ripping open the buttons of his shirt, he tore it off, then reached for his belt.

She moved on the couch as if to go to him,

but he shook his head. She ignored him, lioness that she was, coming to stand before him then dropping to her knees.

'Please,' she said hoarsely, tipping her head back and looking up at him. 'Let me.'

His hunger turned savage. 'Are you sure you want to do that?' He didn't bother to hide the growl in his voice. 'I am in no mood to be kind.'

Silver gleamed in her eyes, as though the sharp edge of the blade she had become was glinting. 'Neither am I.'

This woman was dangerous. She would make a good match for him.

He bared his teeth in a lion's smile. 'Are you hungry for me, little nun? Are you desperate for a taste?'

'Yes.' She lifted her hands, shaking, to his belt buckle. 'So much.'

Dimly, he could feel the king inside him try to take back some control, try to put some distance between him and his hunger. But the king wasn't in charge now.

He was a man and he would have what he wanted.

So he stood there while she undid his belt

and then the fastenings of his trousers, pulling down the zip and opening the two sides. And when she reached inside his boxers to grip the hard length of his shaft, he didn't stop her. Sensation rippled through him as her fingers circled him. She drew him out, sparks of pleasure igniting along all his nerve endings, and another growl was torn from him.

She looked up at him, stroking him, her eyes like moonlight. 'I don't know how to do this. Show me.'

He didn't need to be asked twice. Reaching down, he speared his fingers into the delicate confection of curls on her head, destroying its perfection, and her gasp intensified the pleasure inside him.

'Take me in your mouth,' he ordered.

And she did.

Heat exploded through him, the catch of his breath echoing through the room, fire leaping in her eyes in response. Oh, she liked that. She liked giving him pleasure.

It made him even harder and as her lips closed around him, heat enveloping him, he was trapped by the intensity of her silver gaze, caught in an endless loop of pleasure. She gave him pleasure, and his reaction sparked pleasure in her, which then gave it back to him; it was a constant cycle, an unbreakable current.

She wasn't a nun any longer. She was a lioness, a sword. A goddess kneeling at his feet. And he wanted more, which made his decision to take her for himself the best decision. The only decision.

The man cannot have anything, you know this.

But he discarded that thought as he'd discarded the golden lion pin on his jacket. Tonight, the king was forgotten. There was only the man, and the man had been denied too long.

He told her what to do, but soon she didn't need much in the way of guidance, finding her own way, licking him, tasting him, exploring him, giving little hums of satisfaction every time she drew a growl of pleasure from him, driving him to the brink of insanity.

He pulled her head away from him, ignoring her cry of protest. 'On the couch,' he ordered. And as she did what she was told, he got rid of the rest of his clothes. Then, finally naked, he joined her on the cushions, pushing her rounded thighs wide apart so he could kneel between them.

She was panting, her eyes dark, her skin like silk as he ran his hands all over it.

'Oh... Adonis...please...'

'Beg for me, little nun,' he murmured, his voice nothing but gravel and sand. 'Again.'

And she did, and when he buried his face between her legs, she begged again and again as he tasted her, licking her, exploring all her hidden valleys, all the places she was most sensitive, all the places that gave her the most pleasure, using her cries and sobs as his guide.

Then, when he felt her muscles lock, he slid his hands beneath her bottom and lifted her higher, drinking from her, using his tongue to drive her straight to the edge and then over it.

She arched, convulsing, a cry of ecstasy breaking from her, but he didn't stop, tasting the wild, sweet flavour of her orgasm. Then he slipped one hand between her thighs, stroking through her slippery folds, driving her straight towards another. A choked gasp escaped her, and he shifted, pushing himself up and leaning over her, bending to take one stiff pink nipple in his mouth, sucking hard as he eased one finger inside her, then another, setting up an insistent rhythm of sensation that had her twisting on the sheets and screaming his name yet again as another climax hit her.

He eased her down after that, stroking her as she shuddered through the aftershocks. Strands of hair clung to her damp forehead, her skin gleaming with perspiration, and she looked thoroughly ruined.

But he wasn't done.

You'll never be done.

The thought whispered through his head as he picked her up from the couch cushions, heading for the stairs and the upstairs bedroom, the truth of it settling down into him. No, possibly he wouldn't. But that didn't matter.

She was his now and he'd have all the time in the world to test that theory.

The bed upstairs that faced the windows with the dark sea beyond was wide, the sheets cool, and when he laid her down on it he scanned her face, looking for any signs that she'd had enough.

But when he settled himself between her thighs, her warmth and softness beneath him, she slid her hand into his hair and pulled his head down, her mouth hot and sweet and open under his.

She was so generous. She would never turn him away and he felt the truth of that deep inside him. He could come to her and she would take him in, and she would hold him. He could pour himself into her and she would take it all.

She will put you first.

Something in his chest shifted, something tight. Something he wasn't comfortable with. The embers in the dead hearth of his heart glowed as if someone had breathed air on them.

He ignored it. Instead, he embraced the pleasure as he lifted his head from her mouth and looked into her eyes, thrusting inside her, sheathing himself in her slick heat.

She gasped, his name a prayer on her lips. And when he drew back and thrust again she cried out, her legs closing around his waist, her hips rising to meet his.

And he kept on staring into the silver darkness of her eyes as he drove them both to the edge of oblivion.

And over it.

CHAPTER NINE

ANNA WOKE TO sunlight pressing against her closed lids. She sighed and shifted, conscious that her body ached as if she'd had a hard workout, which was strange, since she wasn't a fan of exercise at the best of times.

Perhaps she'd done too much running around with Ione yesterday?

She shifted again, only to have the large, heavy arm wrapped around her waist tighten, drawing her against something hard and very, very hot.

Her breath caught, shock rippling through her, closely followed by flickers of memory.

Memories of fainting at a ball. Of the king catching her. The king kissing her.

The king inside her, moving with a savage, relentless rhythm, and the cries he'd drawn from her. The pleasure that had coursed through her.

Of looking up into blue eyes gone the colour of midnight, his gaze fierce as it held hers. Moonlight had caught his brutally hand-some features, limning them in silver, and her heart had kicked hard in her chest.

He'd been strong and beautiful and hungry. And he'd kept her awake, demanding more and more of her as the night had gone on. But she hadn't cared. She'd given him everything she had and more, because she was hungry too.

For him and only him.

She kept her eyes closed for a second longer, not wanting to move because there were other memories there apart from pleasure: him telling her that she was pregnant and the future she'd always imagined for herself burning to ashes.

They hadn't discussed anything last night, too caught up in sating the desire that had blazed so intensely between them. She still didn't even know where he'd taken her or why.

Cautiously, she opened her eyes.

They were lying in a big, wide bed, white sheets tumbled and tangled all around them. The bed faced big windows that looked out onto a deep blue ocean, flooding the room with bright sunlight that made the whitewashed stone walls glow.

The dark wood of the floor was covered in

bright silk rugs, another rug pinned to the wall above the bed. It was a simple, bare room, the only furniture the bed, two bedside tables in heavy, dark wood and a carved wooden dresser against one wall.

Clearly, it was the king's house but…where was it? And why had he brought her here?

Moving slowly, she managed to wiggle out from underneath his arm and sat up, turning to look down at him. He was still asleep, the hard lines of his face relaxed, making him seem younger. She stared at the way his mouth curled slightly, as if he was on the verge of a smile.

That would never happen. Adonis didn't smile, or if he did, she'd never seen it.

Her heartbeat gave another kick. She wanted to see it. And she wanted to be the one who made him smile, too, wanted that very much. In fact, there were a lot of things she wanted when it came to him, and it wasn't all about sex, either.

She reached out to touch one heavily muscled shoulder, loving the velvety feel of his warm skin. The lines of his royal tattoo, a crowned lion, stalked across his back, the colours deep and rich, red and gold and black. It was beautiful. She traced the lion's roaring mouth and the edges of its mane, yet another sign that it wasn't just a man lying next to her, but a king.

A king who won't let himself be a man.

'You like that?' The sound of his voice, roughened by the night they'd spent together, took her by surprise, sending a pleasant shock through her.

She almost snatched her hand away, unsure whether she should be taking such liberties. Then again, after last night, surely everything was allowed?

'Yes, it's beautiful.' She touched the gold crown on the lion's head. 'Is it only kings who are allowed the tattoo?'

'Only the crowned lion. Xerxes has one, but his lion doesn't have a crown.'

'When did you get it?'

'When I was eighteen. The royal tattooist is the only one permitted to use this design and only on the royal family. The inks are special too.'

'Will Ione have one?' she asked, curious. 'Or is it only men who have it?'

'Not only men. Ione will have hers when she turns eighteen.' His gaze was clear and cold as a winter sky, focusing intently on her. 'Don't you want to know where we are and why?'

She slid a finger along one of the lion's big paws. 'Tell me.'

'This was my mother's house. My father gave her this island as a wedding present.'

A dark current of emotion threaded through the words and Anna paused in her tracing of the lion on his shoulder, glancing down into his eyes.

His mother. Who'd died in a car accident, according to the history books.

'It seems lovely,' she said carefully.

'It is. She didn't come here much.' He reached suddenly for her hand and took it in his, turning her palm over and studying it intently. 'She preferred the palace. I had a nanny who used to bring me here for holidays.'

Anna shivered as he ran a finger lightly over the centre of her palm, her whole body reacting to his touch. 'A nanny?'

'I didn't spend much time with my parents.' He circled her palm gently, his attention on her hand. 'They were always busy.'

Again there was a dark edge threading through his tone, and it made her throat close in sudden foreboding. The queen had died when he was young... Was this part of his unhappy childhood?

'Your mother died in a car accident, didn't she?' Anna asked hesitantly.

'No,' he said without any discernible emotion. 'It was not a car accident.'

'But wasn't that—'

'A story the media were told. There was no accident. Our car was ambushed by an enemy faction when I was seven. They wanted my father, but he never rode in the same car with us for safety reasons. They overcame our guards, dragged us from the car, and tried to make my mother tell them where he was. But she wouldn't, so they hurt her.'

Anna stared at him, shocked. 'Hurt her?'

'They tortured her, but she wouldn't give away my father's position.' He paused, the icy blue of his eyes fathomless. 'I was desperate to stop them hurting her, so I told them instead.'

Anna's breath caught. 'Oh, Adonis...'

'Even after I'd betrayed the king, she tried to stop them, grabbing one of their guns. But they shot her. My father was injured in the subsequent attack, but luckily his bodyguards were able to save him. My mother died of her injuries.' His voice was so cold, as if it were someone else's mother who'd died, and not his own.

Horror and a terrible sympathy flooded through her. This was the source of the pain she'd seen in his eyes back at the ball, wasn't it? And no wonder. His mother had been tortured right in front of him.

'I'm so sorry,' she whispered. It seemed so empty and inadequate, but it was all she could think of to say.

'My father was furious. He blamed me. Told me that if I'd stayed strong and hadn't given away his position, she wouldn't have grabbed the gun. That the palace guards would have found us and rescued us.'

Anna's throat constricted. 'But you were just a little boy. How could you—'

'It doesn't matter how old I was,' he interrupted harshly. 'I shouldn't have broken. I shouldn't have told them where my father was. I put my feelings for my mother before my duty to protect the throne.' His gaze glittered. 'And she died.'

The look in his eyes made her heart hurt. It was so bleak. So…cold. As if he felt nothing.

Which was a lie, because he did, she knew he did. Last night had proved that, though the mountain might appear icy and remote, inside he was molten. Inside, he was a volcano.

'Adonis...' she began softly.

But he went on, implacable. 'My father was determined to teach me a lesson. He thought I was far too emotional and that enemies would be able to use those emotions against me, so he made it his mission to excise that weakness from me.'

The foreboding that hadn't quite gone away tightened its grip on her.

She didn't want to ask, but then, she didn't need to, because he went on anyway,

'Xenophon kidnapped Xerxes and interrogated him, tortured him. He pretended to be an enemy, using my voice as a way to break my little brother. I was put in the next room and ordered not to intervene. I had to listen to him scream. My will had to be strong enough to withstand him being used as a weapon against me. My first duty was to my throne, not to him.'

Shock washed through her, a bucket of ice water dumped over her head.

This was the reason he was so hard and so cold. She didn't know much about King Xenophon, only that he'd been an old-style king, harsh and militaristic in his ways. But this brutal? Torturing his own sons? Because that was what Adonis was describing. Actual torture. And not only the torture of his brother, but the torture of himself too.

'That's terrible,' she said, an instant and fierce protectiveness rising inside her. Because of what he'd suffered. Because of what his father had put him through. Because of what he'd become. 'That's abuse.'

'It was necessary,' his voice was even icier now, 'because to break would have been to prolong Xerxes's pain.'

'What about your pain?' She knew she sounded demanding, but she was angry and couldn't hide it. 'What kind of father would do that to his own children?'

'He wasn't a father,' Adonis said relentlessly, 'he was a king. Just as I ceased to be his son, only his heir. Emotion can be used as a weapon and so I had to rid myself of it.'

'So that was his excuse?' She couldn't shut herself up. 'That was his justification for hurting you? The fact that emotions can be used against you?'

'He said that our enemies would have no mercy and so he couldn't have any.' Adonis's thick black lashes were a stark contrast to the blue of his eyes. 'He wasn't wrong. Our enemies had no mercy. They tortured my mother because they knew I would break.'

'But that was years ago—'

'Xerxes was captured while on a mission with his platoon,' he interrupted in the same cold tone. 'Our father refused a rescue mission. He was certain Xerxes had been captured in order to draw me out.' A muscle jumped in Adonis's hard jaw. 'I knew I should have put my duty as heir first, but I couldn't let them have my little brother. So I disobeyed my father's orders and mounted a rescue mission. I was successful, but Xenophon wouldn't have any of it. He made me choose once and for all—the throne or exile. He would make Xerxes his heir instead.'

Anna took a shaken breath, fury making it difficult to speak. 'He would have disowned you? Because you rescued your brother?'

Adonis's face remained granite, his eyes hard

jewels. There was no softness in him anywhere. 'A king has to put his country before his feelings. Before his family. Before everything. Besides, exile was kinder to Xerxes than the throne would have been. The lessons my father would have taught him would have destroyed him. I was born for this. It is my duty. I chose to remain his heir.' Adonis paused. 'Xerxes didn't know, but it was that decision that got him banished. My father put him out of my reach once and for all.'

Cold wound through the heat of her anger like a slow-moving frost, cold as the wintry blue of his eyes.

Dear God, the horror of it. No wonder this man was so icy, so hard. He hadn't just learned his father's lessons, he'd become them. They'd turned him to stone.

'I am telling you all of this so that you understand,' Adonis went on, his tone utterly flat. 'A king cannot allow himself to be a man. To feel as a man would. To love as a man would. A king must put his country before everything, even his own family.'

His harshness felt like an arrow to her chest, piercing her. Was that what he was trying to say? That he could have nothing for himself? Nothing for the man? He could have all the power and authority, but there could be no friendship. No laughter. No love.

The nuns might have been distant, but even they had smiled and laughed. Even they had shown her what peace looked like and given her a taste of happiness.

But he hadn't tasted it. He didn't even know what it looked like. How could he? When his father had stripped him of all emotion? His childhood ripped away, a boy tortured for the sake of a throne, and all because of one mistake…

Her eyes pricked with tears, the ferocity of her anger at what had been done to him choking her. 'You know you've been brainwashed, don't you?' she said hoarsely. 'That everything you've been told is a lie?'

An expression rippled across his face, gone too fast for her to tell what it was. 'I brought you here, Anna,' he went on as if she hadn't spoken, 'because first, you are pregnant with my child, and until that resolves itself one way or the other I want you out of harm's way. And second… Ione needs a mother.'

Anna stared at him, her anger forgotten for a moment. 'What?'

His hold on her hand tightened. 'Ione knows you. She likes you, too, which makes you perfect. I want you to be my wife, Anna. Be my queen. Be the mother Ione needs.'

Another wave of shock hit her, stealing any breath remaining in her lungs. 'But…you can't want to marry me. I'm just a nun. I have vows I want to take.'

'You're pregnant. And you can't take your vows if you have a child, most certainly not if that child is mine.' His thumb brushed over the centre of her palm in a sensual stroke that, despite the shock, set all her nerve endings alight. 'And you were right about Ione. She does need more than I can give. You care about her, you put her first.' His gaze was focused, relentless. 'She needs you more than the convent does. More than the Reverend Mother.' Something hotter glittered abruptly in his eyes. 'A convent is not the place for a woman like you, anyway. You're passionate, intense. And I can give you everything you need to satisfy that passion.'

Sex, he was talking about sex. He didn't mean any other kind of passion.

But you want more than that.

Yet the thought was a dim one, hazy, lost under the stunning surprise of his proposal and the vision of a different life that it had conjured up. A life she'd never thought she'd have and yet always wanted.

She could see it now: a husband and child; a family; a place where she belonged.

She'd thought she'd found that in the convent, with God as her husband and her family the church. But now that she considered it, there had always been something…passionless and detached about that vision. Something distant. There was no immediacy to it, no heat. No desire. No laughter and no joy. At least not for her.

There will be no joy with him either, you realise.

Anna stared into his blue eyes, pain winding tight. His childhood had been so bleak, abusive even. He wouldn't even know what joy was. But if there was ever someone who needed to learn, it was him. His father had brainwashed him into thinking his emotions were the enemy, but if he could learn how to isolate himself, he could also unlearn it. He'd already given in to the passion inside him, so perhaps he could also allow himself other things. Such as happiness and warmth. Joy and laughter.

Love.

And why not love? Who loved him? His brother did, but that was a sibling's love. His daughter loved her father, yes, and his people loved the king, but who loved the man?

You can.

The thought had sharp edges, cutting her in places that were far too vulnerable and exposed, but she ignored them. Yes, she could love him. That was possible. No, it was necessary. He hadn't had enough love in his life from the sounds of it, and he needed it. And so did his little girl. He had no one else to give it to him. No one but her.

And the convent? Your vows?

He was right; the convent didn't need her. She'd never fitted in there anyway. And the Reverend Mother had been right, too, to send her to Axios, to a king desperate for what she had so much of to give: love.

And what about you? Don't you need it?

The warning was loud in her head because if he couldn't put his daughter before his country, then he would never put *her* first. He would never give her in return what she could give him.

But maybe that didn't matter. She'd gone years without it, and he had passion at least. Maybe in time that would change. And there was Ione to think about as well…

Was it even a choice?

'Yes,' she said, her voice only a little rough, staring into those cold, implacable blue eyes. 'Yes, I will be your wife.'

The fire in his gaze leapt high. He let go of her hand, his arms coming around her, drawing her in against him, into his heat. Then he turned them both and she found herself lying beneath him, caged by heat, hard muscle, and smooth, velvety skin.

He was above her, his piercing gaze holding her captive. 'Then you'll be mine, little nun. And in return you will be queen, your nights full of all the pleasure I can give you, and your days spent with a little girl who desperately needs you. You have a home with me at the palace, I swear it.'

You will be his. But he will never be yours.

A shudder moved through her, a fault line inside her reminding her that there were cracks in her heart. Cracks that hadn't healed and perhaps never would.

But it didn't matter. Her heart, cracked or not, was big enough for all of them.

Conviction settled down inside her as she looked up into his strong face. Yes, she was here for a reason and that reason wasn't just a small, excitable girl, but a man. A king. A lonely mountain who needed someone, even if that mountain didn't know it yet himself.

And she knew that the vows she was meant to take were never supposed to be ones of chastity and sacrifice, and her vocation wasn't to be part of the church. Her vows were those of marriage, and her vocation was to be with him. He was her church and she was meant to worship him.

She didn't speak.

Instead she reached up and pulled him down, taking her first communion from his mouth.

Adonis decided not to return to the palace that day. Or indeed the next. Or even the one after that. Instructing Xerxes to take over for a couple of days, he didn't bother with an explanation, merely telling his surprised brother that he was taking some time off. He also issued another order for Ione to be brought to the island after a couple of days, allowing himself and Anna to have some time together before they broke the news of their impending wedding to the little girl.

He told himself that keeping Anna with him was necessary because they needed to discuss how a marriage between them would work, nothing at all to do with the raw possessiveness that gripped him, making it impossible to keep his hands off her.

They spent that first day in bed, disturbed only by palace staff arriving with clothing and personal items for them both, not to mention stocking the place with food. And then the staff left, leaving them entirely alone.

So he indulged himself with her. Indulged himself utterly. She'd left his detachment in ruins the night she'd fainted in his arms, and since it had shattered so completely there wasn't any point in rebuilding it. Not yet at least.

There would be plenty of time for that later, when they returned to the palace, and in the meantime he might as well let himself be a man for a little while. It was temporary. He'd rebuilt himself once before; he could do so again. And besides, if he gave his hunger for her free rein, perhaps it would ease their intense physical chemistry.

She certainly took delight in the lessons he gave her on how to please him, taking to them with relish and enthusiasm, cementing his opinion that the convent was not and had never been the place for her. She had far too much passion to lead the quiet life of celibacy required of a nun, and it made him rethink his position on the Reverend Mother sending her to him.

Perhaps his godmother knew more than he'd initially thought.

While he demanded her passion during the day, in the evenings he decided to cement their relationship further by cooking for her, much to her shock, which amused him. In fact, shocking her for his own amusement was getting to be moderately addictive, and, since she was getting harder to shock in bed, he found he had to demonstrate his talents elsewhere.

Cooking was one of those talents. His nanny had taught him right here in this very kitchen, with the scrubbed wooden table and herbs, and pots and pans hanging from a wooden frame above it. She'd been of the opinion that a man needed a few practical skills and being able to feed himself was one of the most basic. Xenophon hadn't approved, but Adonis had learned all the same, and discovered he had quite the talent for it.

Since ascending the throne, he never got a chance to cook, and rather to his own surprise he found himself appreciating the opportunity to do so now. Especially with Anna sitting at the table opposite him, watching him chop onions with wide eyes, making him want to show off like a thirteen-year-old boy in front of a girl he had a crush on.

'I can't believe you can cook,' she said in awed tones.

'My nanny taught me. She was a firm believer in a man being able to look after himself.'

Anna took a sip of the orange juice he'd poured for her, leaning her chin in one hand, watching him. 'You enjoy it, don't you?'

Did he? He never did anything for his own enjoyment, because his own enjoyment was never paramount. Yet...there was something about creating sustenance for her that pleased him.

'There is something meditative about working with your hands,' he admitted.

Her eyes gleamed. 'I know how you can work with your hands.'

He smiled. Her fledgling attempts at flirtation were adorable. 'What a naughty nun you are. Perhaps after dinner I can show you a few other things I can do with my hands.'

She flushed beautifully, her mouth turning up. 'Perhaps I'll even let you.' Her gaze flickered to the flash of his knife on the chopping board and her smile faded. 'I never learned how to cook. The nuns wouldn't let me near the kitchen.'

There was a wistful note in her voice, making him pause in his chopping to stare at her lovely face. 'You sound unhappy about that.'

'Oh?' She looked a little surprised. 'Do I?'

'Yes.'

'I don't mean to. I suppose I was only thinking about how lovely it was that you had someone to teach you.' She let out a breath, but didn't offer more.

He put the knife down, unable to tear his gaze from the flicker of sadness in her grey eyes. She'd been fostered with the nuns, or so she'd told him that night in his office, which meant that she wouldn't have had a family. And it was clear from the look on her face now that she felt the lack acutely.

It made his chest tighten with sympathy.

You feel the lack of yours too.

But how could he? He'd never had a family. All he'd had was a training regime.

'You've been brainwashed... Everything you've been told is a lie...'

'I know you were fostered by the nuns,' he said, shoving that memory aside, 'but did you ever make contact with your parents?'

Her smile vanished, her gaze dropping to the table top. 'I couldn't find my father. But I tracked my mother down a couple of years ago and yes, I made contact with her. I emailed her a few times, talked to her on the phone.' Anna traced a small line in the condensation on the sides of her glass. 'She seemed nice enough.'

He frowned, caught by the edge in her tone. 'And?'

Her head tilted, her concentration on the glass. 'I wanted to meet her and she told me she wanted to meet me too. So I tried to orga-nise a few meetings, but when the time came she would always cancel. I asked her why and she told that me that she already had a family and didn't want to rake up the past again. Then she broke off all contact.' Her voice grew tight. 'I understood. It was hard for her.'

His own muscles tightened too because, while Anna might have said she understood, it was clear the rejection had struck her somewhere vulnerable deep inside. And he disliked the thought of her in pain. He disliked it intensely.

'But you were hurt nonetheless,' he said, not making it a question.

Anna lifted a shoulder as if that wasn't relevant. 'She'd had a hard life. It made sense that she didn't want to have it all brought back to her.'

He noted the tension around her mouth and jaw. 'Except you wanted to meet her, didn't you?' He wasn't sure why he was pushing for information, especially since it was obviously an old wound and he didn't want to reopen it, not to mention that her pain made him uncomfortable. But he couldn't ignore it, either.

She gave another small sigh. 'I would have liked to. I just…wanted to make contact with someone who was related to me, to see where

I came from, that kind of thing. I felt out of place in the convent, so I wanted to know if I perhaps belonged elsewhere.' She made a dismissive gesture. 'But my mother was uncomfortable with that and so I let it go. It's fine.'

But it wasn't fine and he could see that.

'Your mother might have had her reasons for not wanting to keep in contact with you, Anna, but that doesn't make it any less a rejection. Especially one you didn't deserve.'

'That's the issue though. Perhaps I did deserve it. I wasn't very nice to her, you see. I told her that she owed me a meeting after getting rid of me and then she got upset and hung up on me.' Anna sat back, her hands in her lap, and her shoulders hunched. 'I shouldn't have got so angry with her. It was the wrong thing to do.'

He could hear the bitterness in her tone, saw the hurt radiating from her. And he'd moved around the table towards her before he was even conscious of doing so.

She lifted her head as he approached, resisting slightly as he pulled her from the chair she was sitting in. But as soon as he put his arms around her, she melted utterly against him and put her forehead on his chest.

'I made a stupid mistake, Adonis,' she said, her voice muffled in his T-shirt. 'I shouldn't have got so angry. I just wanted so badly to talk to her, to have some kind of connection with her. To know where I came from and who my family was. And why she didn't want me. What was so wrong with me that...' Anna broke off, her small body shivering.

And he felt that shift in his chest again, a tight sensation that wouldn't let up, and he didn't like it. He didn't know where the impulse to take her in his arms had come from either. But he didn't release her. She was upset and in pain and it felt wrong to leave her to deal with it alone. She was also warm and holding on to him, clinging to him, calling to the deep protectiveness that had woken when he'd found out about her pregnancy.

'There's nothing wrong with you.' He put a comforting hand on the back of her head, letting his palm rest against her pale, silky hair. 'You know that, don't you?'

'Mum didn't want me, not even years later. And I was always such a trial to the nuns. I don't think they wanted me either—'

He reached for her chin, forcing her head

back so she had to look up at him. Her eyes were full of hurt and a bitterness that he hated to see there. 'It's not you. How could it be? Your mother didn't even know the woman you grew up to be.' He let her see the conviction burning in his eyes. 'And as for the nuns, the Reverend Mother knew your worth. Why else did she send you to help Ione? You're unselfish and generous. Warm and passionate. You're exactly what Ione needs.'

Anna's eyes gleamed with tears, but there was something else in the look she gave him that made the tightness in his chest contract even further. 'And you?' she asked. 'What about what you need?'

You need her.

The thought was bright and burning, making longing curl through him. Anna, warm and generous and giving. Anna, who'd braved his disapproval in order to help Ione.

Anna, who'd never put a throne before a person.

The way your parents did?

'You shouldn't ask me questions like that, little nun. Not when you know the answer already,' he said, his voice unaccountably rough, ignoring that thought. Of course his parents had put the throne before their son. They'd *had* to.

She didn't look away, and he had the disturbing impression that she could see inside him, see all the thoughts in his head.

'I wasn't asking the king,' she said quietly. 'I was asking you.'

He lifted his hands and cupped her face between them, keeping his touch gentle, because his words would not be. 'Anna. You know this already. I can't be anything other than the king. And a king can't need anyone.'

Her gaze searched his face and the strange, tight feeling inside him grew. 'I know that's what your father made you believe. But it's not true.'

'Anna—'

'Do you think I can only be a nun? That I can't be a friend as well? Or that Xerxes can only be a prince and not a father?'

It felt as if she'd found a vulnerability in his armour and had slid a knife inside it, cutting him. 'It's different for you. Different for him,' he said flatly, not wanting to discuss it.

'Why?' She threw the question at him like

a stone. 'How? You're a man like Xerxes is. You're also a father.'

'A king has to protect millions—'

'Stop spouting the lies your father taught you, Adonis,' she interrupted, suddenly fierce. 'Because that's what they are. Lies. Not having emotion doesn't make you a king, it makes you a robot.' Her eyes glittered. 'It makes you him.'

He dropped his hands from her face and took a step back, his heart beating far too fast and he wasn't sure why. He wasn't his father, of course he wasn't. Xenophon had been brutal, yes, but everything he'd done had been to help Adonis be a better king.

It had been for Axios's sake.

It's always about Axios. Never about you.

'I'm not him,' he growled. 'If I were, do you think I would have asked you to marry me? I would not do to Ione what was done to me.'

'And yet you hold her at a distance. You tell her you have no time. And you tell yourself that the throne comes first.' Concern flooded her lovely face along with a sympathy that cut him open. 'Is that what your father told you, too? That he couldn't put you first? That the throne came before everything?'

Pain throbbed inside him, a crack running through his soul.

His mother had held out despite how those men had tortured her, but not to protect him. It had been for her husband. To protect the king. Then she'd taken that gun, bringing about her own death, and it had all been to protect the throne. Not to save her son.

And his father hadn't seemed to care how the blame he'd laid on his oldest son for his mother's death had crushed him. How the torture of his little brother had torn him apart.

The throne was more important. It was always about the throne.

But how could it be about anything else? A country and the lives of millions were always going to be more important than he was.

'He was right,' Adonis forced out, hearing his own father's voice in the words and hating the sound of it. Hating himself for saying it. 'The throne has to come first.'

She lifted her hand and cupped his cheek before he could pull away, her touch warm as sunlight. 'You can't believe that.'

But he did. The love he'd once had for his father had died a death the day Xerxes had been banished, yet he still carried the spirit of Xenophon's teachings.

'You don't understand,' he said roughly. 'I *have* to believe it. Otherwise everything that was done to me, to Xerxes, would have been for nothing.'

There was such sadness in her eyes. 'That's the bleakest thing I've ever heard.'

He could feel tension crawling through every part of him and he had to concentrate to hold himself still. 'What do you want from me, Anna?'

She stared at him and he didn't know what she was looking for. 'I don't want anything from you. I just want you to know that you're not alone.'

He couldn't have said why that felt like a knife twisting inside him, cutting him deeper, but it did, a sharp, insistent pain.

He didn't like it. And he didn't want to talk about this any more. So he kissed her hard instead, ending the conversation.

CHAPTER TEN

ANNA SAT ON the end of the small jetty that projected out from the rocky beach of the island and into the deep blue water. The sun was warm on her back and she had her feet dangling in the cool water.

In the small, sheltered cove, a little sailboat tacked back and forth, its white sail shining in the sun. She could hear Ione's shrieks of delight echo across the water as her father guided the small boat, and a bittersweet feeling collected inside her.

Ione had arrived a couple of days earlier and had greeted the news that her father was going to marry Anna with a great deal of satisfaction.

'Good,' Ione had said. 'I didn't want you to leave. Marrying Papa means you have to stay.'

They'd spent the past few days adjusting to the new state of things, not that Ione seemed to require much adjustment. Not when she'd spent most of the time basking in the attention from not just one, but two adults.

When Ione had first arrived, Adonis had been stiff and unbending, as if he didn't quite know how to treat her, not helped by the fact that Ione had been a bit manic to start off with. But then, when she realised that her father wasn't suddenly going to send her away as he did in the palace, she settled down and relaxed, and little by little so did he.

Anna didn't know what had changed, whether it was being away from the palace and his duties, or whether it had something to do with the conversation she'd tried to have with him about his father, or perhaps it was simply having some time with his daughter, but Adonis seemed different.

He became less expressionless, less cold. A granite statue became warm, living flesh. A king slowly turned back into a man.

He joined in the activities Anna had organised: picnics and swimming and fishing off the end of the jetty, then stories and games in the evenings, and walking along the beach finding seashells during the day.

One night he'd smiled at her and it had taken

her breath away. Then the next, he'd laughed at something Ione had said and the sound had made her heart squeeze tight in her chest.

Today he'd readied the small boat kept in a little shed by the water, deciding to take Ione for a sail. Sailing was something he'd learned from his nanny and, considering the casual competence with which he handled the boat, it was obvious he'd once spent a lot of time out on the water.

But watching him with his daughter made Anna ache.

Did he know he was a different man out here, on the island? Was he aware at all?

He was so unbelievably handsome when he became human. So charismatic. A king anyone would follow. A king anyone would die for.

'You don't understand, I have to believe it...'

Her throat contracted at the memory of his voice and the ferocity in his eyes as she'd confronted him about his father, about those lessons Xenophon had taught him. Lessons in torture and pain. Lessons in abuse.

She could only guess at his father's motives, and she had no idea whether Xenophon had truly believed that he was helping Adonis be a better king or whether he had been punishing his son for his mother's death—or perhaps even punishing himself for failing to save his wife. But maybe that didn't matter. What mattered was that Adonis felt he had to believe his father.

She put her hand up over her eyes to shield them from the sun as she looked out over the sea to where the little boat sailed. It was the sun that made her eyes water, surely, not the memory of him looking down into her eyes and cupping her face between his hands, telling her that there was nothing wrong with her, that she was a great many wonderful things. And that she was needed.

He wasn't detached, no matter what he said. And he didn't believe what his father had taught him, not deep down, she was sure of it. Why else would he hold her so gently? And give her such reassurance?

Why else would he be worrying so much about his brother, even now?

'Everything Xerxes went through would have been for nothing...'

He carried guilt for his brother's torture at their father's hands; she'd seen it in his eyes. Guilt for his mother's death, too, and no doubt guilt for his own treatment of his daughter as well. No wonder he clung to his father's lies and detached himself so completely from his own emotions. They must have caused him such agony.

Anna blinked the moisture from her eyes, a ghost of that agony echoing inside herself.

Knowing all of this didn't change anything, though. She'd wanted him to know that he wasn't alone, and that was still true.

But what you feel for him...

She knew what she felt for him. She'd known it for days. Perhaps she'd even known it for weeks, ever since the night he'd made love to her in his office.

The decision she'd made the first morning here had taken hold: she'd fallen for him completely and utterly, and with no hope of return.

Not that falling for him changed anything either. No, it only made her even more certain that what she was doing was the right thing.

He was a lonely man with deep wounds and he needed healing, but they hadn't talked about his father again, and the only connection with her he'd allowed was in bed, in that room overlooking the sea.

It was a start. She only hoped it would be enough of one.

Anna's throat felt sore as the little boat turned towards the jetty, the waves glittering in the afternoon sun, and began to make its way back to shore.

Ten minutes later the boat was tied up, and Ione had leapt off, chattering at Anna about how she was going to be a pirate queen when she grew up and make people walk the plank. Adonis, leaping off after her, laughed and in a completely natural movement reached down to swing her up onto his shoulders, telling her that she would make a superb pirate, though he wasn't sure about the plank-walking.

The pain in Anna's throat worsened at the show of spontaneous physical affection, and not only that, but there was also laughter in his voice and in his eyes, his beautiful mouth turning up into a smile that took her breath away.

This was the man he should be. A man who looked as though he knew happiness. Who was relaxed and smiling, warmth radiating from him as he reached out his hand to her, and they all walked up the path to the house above the sea.

Not the hard, granite-faced king, but this

charming, charismatic man. The man he would never allow himself to be.

It won't happen. He won't let it.

No, it had to happen. And if she loved him enough, he might…

They spent another couple of magical days on the island, Anna shoving aside her growing trepidation at returning to the mainland, trying to remain optimistic that the happiness they'd discovered as a small family would remain even after they'd returned to the palace.

Yet when the day came that they had to leave, and they were all in the helicopter flying back to Itheus, the trip was a silent one; even Ione was quiet. And the closer they got to the palace, the more Anna felt Adonis withdrawing. His features hardened, his powerful body tensing, those blue eyes becoming sharper, cutting. The smile vanished and his mouth became hard and unyielding.

The man he'd been on the island disappeared so completely it was as if he'd never existed.

She had no time to speak with him when they landed. The instant he got out of the helicopter he was surrounded by people, and he didn't look at her or Ione once as they exited behind him. He didn't glance around to see if they were coming; he simply strode along the path to the palace, deep in conversation with his aides.

Anna had hoped some sign of the man would remain, but it hadn't.

The man was gone. All that was left was the king.

It felt like a knife in her heart.

More palace staff surrounded her, and as Ione was led off Anna was taken back not to the little room she'd once occupied, and not to the king's personal suite either, but to another suite of rooms in the wing where the royal family lived.

The bedroom was large and airy, with big windows that looked out over Itheus and a stone balcony to take advantage of the magnificent view. A huge four-poster bed, hung with gauzy white curtains, stood against one wall, angled towards the windows, while other carved, heavy furniture was scattered about.

It was luxurious and beautiful, but a chill had settled down inside her and she couldn't get rid of it. She didn't know why she'd been put here. Surely, she would now be sleeping with

Adonis? Then again, maybe not. Maybe he was trying to keep a sense of propriety.

She tried to ignore the cold feeling, busying herself with settling in and then going to see if Ione was okay. The little girl had been fractious and tired, only wanting to watch TV and not do anything else, which was unusual, since she was normally very active. Her nannies were puzzled by this behaviour, but Anna wasn't. She knew that Ione was feeling exactly the way she was feeling too because she wouldn't see her father again, not the way he had been back on the island.

Anna did what she could for her, and later that evening tucked her into bed with a story, but Adonis didn't come to say goodnight the way he'd done every night in that house by the sea, and he didn't send a message.

And when she went back to her own rooms she found a meal had been laid out for her on the coffee table, but it hadn't been made by him and he wasn't sitting there waiting for her, smiling. There was no one there at all.

He had become the mountain again: icy, remote and completely inaccessible.

She told herself that it was okay, that, now

he'd experienced what it was like to have a real family, he would start to let down his guard again. It would just take some time.

But, deep down, a part of her doubted.

The next couple of days were the same. She didn't see him, and when she asked where he was she was told that the king was catching up on work and was very busy.

Of course he was busy. He was always busy. Not that she had nothing to do herself. Wedding preparations were happening and there were dress-designer appointments and make-up consultations, plans for her hair and for the flowers she would carry, a meeting with the Archbishop of Axios, who would conduct the ceremony in Itheus's big cathedral.

But no Adonis. And no message from him either.

She tried not to let that bother her. Tried to tell herself that of course there would be a period of adjustment. That he would find his way back to her and to the man he'd been on the island again in time, she just had to be patient. In the meantime, she flung herself into caring for Ione to distract herself from the insistent, dragging doubt that the little family she'd been part of so briefly would always be missing one of its most vital components.

Him.

Five days later, alone in the luxurious rooms he'd set aside for her, Anna pushed wide the doors to the balcony and stumbled outside, feeling inexplicably as if she couldn't breathe.

She'd had a day of dress fittings and Ione being difficult, and there was a sadness inside her that she couldn't escape. It dragged at her, pulled at her, made her bad tempered, and the brittle calm she'd been trying to maintain had broken. She'd spoken too sharply to Ione, making the little girl run from her in tears, and making herself feel as if she were right back in the convent, desperate for something she couldn't name.

The night was deep and warm and velvety, the lights of the city beneath the palace glittering, the mountains looming on either side. The air was cool on her skin, but not too cold, carrying with it the memory of the hot noonday sun.

It was a beautiful night, but Anna couldn't

enjoy it, unable to shake the sense that she'd only swapped one empty place for another, and both of those places were missing something vital. Something that could have made them home. Something she could never have.

She stood at the parapet and put her hands on the cool stone, taking breath after breath. Perhaps it was simply panic about the wedding and becoming queen. An attack of bridal nerves…

It's him you're missing. It's him you'll never have.

Cold iced the blood in her veins, doubt hooking its claws into her, and she had to take yet another breath to get control of it.

Yes, she was missing him. But she had to be patient. Had to believe that he would eventually come to see that what he'd found on the island he could have here too.

Ione was only tired and so was she. Tomorrow would be better. Perhaps she might even see him. That would help. She didn't need much, just his presence somewhere close by.

Behind her came the sound of her bedroom door shutting, and when she turned it felt as if her heart had stopped beating and was seizing in her chest.

Adonis was striding towards her, tall and powerful, shrugging out of his suit jacket and discarding it on the couch as he came. Pulling at the grey tie around his neck and jerking that off too, he tossed it negligently onto the floor, leaving him wearing a black business shirt and charcoal suit trousers that highlighted his strength and dark, masculine power, making every feminine sense she had sit up and take notice. His expression was stony, but the blue of his eyes burned like a gas flame.

Had he remembered their time on the island? Was he coming to tell her that was what he wanted? Was he coming to tell her that he needed her?

But he didn't say a word and he didn't look anywhere else but at her, coming across the room and through the double doors that led out onto the balcony. And he didn't stop. He reached for her and pulled her into his arms. He lifted his hands, sliding his fingers into her hair, tipping her head back and covering her mouth, hard and demanding.

It was a hungry, frantic kiss, echoing the hunger and demand in her own heart, crushing the doubt, melting the ice.

That man was still there. Her lover of the island. She could taste the desperation in his kiss, the longing for something more, the need for a connection.

It was there and perhaps it would take a long time for him to say it, or perhaps he never would, but that didn't mean he didn't feel it. That didn't mean he didn't want it.

She couldn't doubt him or put her own fears before what was in her heart.

His parents might not have put him first, but she would.

He needed her to and so she'd give him everything. Whatever he wanted, anything at all. She would give him all of it. Her mind. Her heart. Her soul.

Anna melted against him the way he'd been dreaming of for days now. Her mouth was open and hot under his, her lush curves pressed to every inch of him.

Since getting back from the island, he'd had a mountain of work to get through, because, although Xerxes had handled most of it, there was always more, and there were some things he alone had to do.

Adonis had informed Xerxes of his intention to marry and had installed Anna in new rooms in the family wing of the palace. To say Xerxes had been surprised was an understatement. But Adonis hadn't been in the mood to discuss that, or the child Anna was carrying, and so he'd sent his brother away and buried himself in his work.

Or, at least, he'd tried, starting with rebuilding the detachment he'd left in ruins back on the island.

Yet for some reason he couldn't. Because every time he attempted to detach himself from his emotions, all he could think about was walking along the beach and the leap of joy in his heart as Ione had put her hand in his; the tenderness that had filled him as Anna lay against him in the dark; the satisfaction of cooking for her; the happiness as he'd tacked across the bay in the little yacht, with Ione laughing in the sun…

The happiness that had ruined him.

That was why it was impossible to put his

emotions aside, why he couldn't shake the coiling, tangling need that had clawed at him ever since he'd returned to the palace.

He'd tasted happiness and now he wanted more.

He'd thought denial would work, that his will would be strong enough, that if he stayed away from Anna, he would be able to hold out. But all those years of his father's training apparently hadn't been enough, because the instant he'd had an evening free he'd left his office and made straight for her rooms.

He was weak, the way his father had always told him he was.

Adonis kissed her deeper, harder, the hunger inside him seeming to get more intense with every passing second. And there was no point resisting it now, so he didn't.

Anna shuddered against him, her arms around his neck, letting him devour her, letting him ravage her mouth like a conqueror.

She tasted like heaven and he was so hard he couldn't think, let alone resist.

Picking her up in his arms, he turned from the balcony, striding back into the room. He laid her down on the bed, pulling off the silky white nightgown she wore and exposing all that beautiful soft pale skin. He got rid of his own clothes in seconds flat and then he was on the bed with her, pushing apart her thighs. She gasped as he slid a hand between them, stroking the hot, silky flesh he found there, making her writhe, readying her for him. But only when she was slick and trembling did he settle himself between her legs.

She reached for him without hesitation, and when he thrust hard into her she groaned and closed her legs around him, holding him tight to her in welcome. And then there was nothing but the building hunger, the feel of her around him, slippery and soft, her pulse beating fast and frantic in the hollow of her throat.

This is it. This is happiness. With her.

Her eyes were very dark as they looked up into his, pleasure glittering there, and the truth caught at his heart, fierce and bright, like embers exploding into flames.

Yes, *this* was happiness. *She* was happiness. She was what he'd wanted all this time. What he'd needed and never known.

What you can never have.

But he couldn't deal with that thought, not

now, so he tried to drown it with pleasure, taking her to the brink of climax over and over again, keeping her hovering, almost but not quite tipping over.

She trembled and shook beneath him, her nails digging into his shoulders, his name a ragged prayer. The bright, fierce heat he felt in his own heart glowed in her eyes, and, when he drove her over the edge and ecstasy rippled over her lovely face, it flared, making her gaze glitter as brightly as stars, illuminating her from within.

He couldn't look at her, so he kissed her savagely instead as he took his own pleasure in hard, deep thrusts, letting the orgasm take him, letting the ecstasy annihilate him.

But there was no escape. Even when he closed his eyes the truth was still there, the fire burning hot in the hearth of his heart—the hearth that was supposed to stay dead and cold, but hadn't.

This is what your father was protecting you from.

Yes, he understood now. Of course his father hadn't shown mercy. Of course he'd been brutal and hard. Because happiness was a drug, and once you'd had a taste, all you wanted was more.

Xenophon had known his son too well, had known how hot Adonis's emotions burned. How he'd always wanted more. He'd wanted his mother to protect him, not his father's position, not the throne. And he'd wanted his father to comfort him after she'd died, not blame him. And when his father had made him choose between being a son and being an heir, he'd wanted to be a son. But how could he choose that when Xenophon had only wanted an heir?

His emotions were the problem. His need to be put before everything, his need for love. Because Xenophon had known, even if Adonis hadn't, that his son would always put that need before everything else.

And he had. He could have stopped Xerxes's torture, could have protected him, but he'd let it go on, because he'd wanted his father's approval. He'd wanted his love. Perhaps he'd even betrayed his parents all those years ago out of anger. Because he'd wanted to be put first, and he never had been…

His heartbeat was far too fast, the heat of his

orgasm dissipating, leaving behind it a creeping, icy sensation.

Love was the problem. Love was the mistake. And he could feel it burning in his chest—love for the woman lying under him, so deep and intense and fierce. And he knew if he gave in to it, he would end up doing anything for her.

Even betraying a nation the way he'd done years ago.

He couldn't do that. He couldn't give in. Which meant there was only one option, only one choice. The same choice his father had always given him.

Son or heir? Brother or crown? Love or country?

He chose the throne. He always chose the throne.

Adonis shoved himself away from the woman on the bed, rolling off it and getting to his feet. His blood rushed through his veins, his pulse loud in his head. He couldn't get enough air.

'Adonis?' Her voice was soft and he could hear concern in it. Concern for him.

He turned and there she was, sitting up on the bed, completely naked, her hair around her shoulders and gleaming softly in the dim light of the room. Concern shone in her face, because that was the kind of woman she was. Unselfish and giving. Honest and open.

A woman he couldn't allow himself to have, no matter how badly he wanted her.

His emotions could put an entire nation in danger and he couldn't allow that. And, since he hadn't been able to resist her, the only thing he could do was send her away.

As his brother had been sent away.

There were tears in her eyes. 'You're going to send me away, aren't you?'

Of course she knew. She could read him like no one else. She could read every thought in his head.

'I have to,' he said, because there was no point in denial.

'Are you going to tell me why?' Her chin took on a determined slant. 'But don't feed me the same lies your father told you. I don't believe them.'

Pain crawled through him, aching and raw, his need for her tightening his fists and eating at his heart. 'Because I love you.' The words weren't a blessing. They were a curse.

Shock flickered over her lovely face and then

came joy, lighting her up like a Roman candle. She threw aside the sheet, sliding from the bed, apparently not caring that she was naked. Her skin glowed like pearls, her eyes like fine silver, glittering and precious as she came to him.

But he threw up a hand, stopping her in her tracks. He couldn't let her get close, otherwise he would break. And he wasn't going to break, not again. 'But I can't love you, Anna,' he said harshly. 'That's why you have to go.'

A fierce expression shone in her face. 'If you can't love me, then don't. I didn't ask you to. Just don't send me away.'

Of course his little nun would protest. Except this was the best decision for her too. He could cut out this love he felt; he could survive its loss. But she wouldn't. She was an orchid, in need of heat and light and care, and there was only darkness and coldness where he was. She would end up withering and dying, and she deserved more than that.

'No,' he said, his voice icy. 'Regardless of whether you asked for love or not, you need it, Anna. You cannot survive without it.'

'That's not true—'

'Tell me I'm wrong, then. Tell me you haven't

been searching your whole life for someone who will love you the way your mother didn't. The way the nuns in your convent couldn't.'

She flushed, her eyes glittering. 'What does that matter? I don't have to get that love from you.'

'Then where will you get it? From whom? From Ione? That's a child's love. What about at night, when you want someone to hold you—'

'Don't make this about me,' she interrupted fiercely. 'This is about you. You want love, Adonis. You want it so badly, but you won't let yourself have it. You won't let yourself take it.' Her eyes glowed so bright, like stars. 'I love you. And I'll wait for you. I'll wait as long as it takes for you to realise that you can have what you want: joy, laughter, happiness… Everything you never had, everything you want, it's yours.'

He did want it. He wanted it so badly that if he moved, even a step, it would be to take her in his arms.

She will fail you in the end. They all fail you…

And that was true, wasn't it? His mother had put her husband first and his father his throne.

They hadn't cared about what happened to him. No one had.

He'd told himself Xenophon had only been trying to make him into a better king, helping him to protect his country, and that maybe, deep down, his father was doing it because he cared.

But those were lies, just as Anna had said.

His father hadn't cared about him. He'd just wanted him to do what he was told.

And now here was Anna, telling him she loved him, that she'd give him everything he ever wanted. But…how could he trust that? How could he trust that one day something or someone else wouldn't become more important to her than he was?

He couldn't. He wouldn't. Detachment was better than that pain any day.

Besides, when there was a choice, he chose the throne. That at least was familiar.

'No,' he said coldly, surrounding himself in ice and stone. 'I'm sorry, Anna. It's you or the crown and the crown always wins.'

The pretty flush that had stained her skin slowly dissipated, the joy leaving her eyes. She looked hollowed out and far too pale. 'You're not going to change your mind, are you?' Her voice was only a whisper. 'You'll never change your mind. He did his work far too well.'

A crack opened up inside him, yawning wide, pain pressing at the edges.

He ignored it, turning away and picking up his shirt from where he'd thrown it, anything to distract himself, to get himself under control.

'And Ione?' Anna asked huskily when he didn't speak. 'If you can't love me, then you can't love her. Will you send her away too?'

'I'll find someone else to fulfil your role.' He kept his voice hard as he pulled on the shirt and then the rest of his clothes.

'Will you bring her up to be like you?' Anna went on implacably. 'Will you crush her spirit? Torture people she cares about so she learns to detach herself as well? Make sure she never knows joy or happiness or love?'

He whirled back to face her, shirt still open, his heart racing. 'Enough!'

But somehow Anna had come closer and she was standing in front of him, small and beautiful and naked. And her hands reached for him, cupping his face. 'Don't become him,' she said hoarsely. 'Don't become your father. If not for my sake, at least for hers.'

Her touch burned, fire against his skin, the pain in her eyes reaching into his soul and wrenching him apart.

Isn't she right? Isn't that what you've become?

Perhaps she was right. Perhaps this had been his destiny all along.

He took her wrists gently in his fingers, pulling her hands from his face even as he buried the pain in his heart. 'I won't hurt her, I swear it.'

'That's not what I asked.' Her gaze searched his, a sharp, bright grief in her eyes. 'He failed you, Adonis. And he failed your brother too.'

A thread of agony crawled through him, despite the ice, but it was the agony of the man and so he crushed it. Crushed it utterly.

He didn't want to be the man any longer.

He needed to be the king.

'No, Anna,' he said without expression, getting rid of his emotions once and for all. 'Don't you see? He saved me. Without him, I would never have had the strength to send you away.'

Tears tracked down her cheeks in shiny silver trails, but she didn't look away from him.

'That's not strength, that's fear,' she said, her voice broken and yet firm. 'But I suppose you'll never understand that, will you?'

'No, little nun,' he said gently. 'I won't.'

More tears slid down her face, but she didn't bother wiping them away. 'Fine. But what happens to our baby?'

A whisper of pain echoed through him, a ghost of that possessiveness, so faint he could hardly feel it.

'You will be monitored,' he said. 'The child will be provided for, whatever happens.'

She remained standing there, her back straight, her chin lifted. 'I meant what I said. I'll always love you, Adonis Nikolaides. And if one day you wake up and realise that you do want me after all, I'll be waiting for you.'

Deep down, where the man lay buried beneath the rock and ice of the king, a tremor shook him.

But he'd made his choice. And he wouldn't choose again.

'Don't wait,' he said coldly. 'Never is a long time.'

Then he turned on his heel and walked out.

CHAPTER ELEVEN

ANNA THOUGHT ABOUT going to bed, but she knew she wouldn't sleep. It felt as though her heart had broken into a thousand jagged pieces in her chest and she couldn't stop the tears from streaming down her cheeks.

But they weren't tears for herself. They were for him. For the man she'd watched slowly and relentlessly become encased in stone and ice. For the burning flame in his blue eyes that was snuffed out, to be replaced by a cold, jewel-bright glitter.

He was becoming the king. Becoming his father.

And she'd been wrong. He hadn't come to his senses at all. He'd told her he loved her and, far from that being the thing that brought him to her, it had only driven him away.

He was afraid; she could see that now. Afraid of what he felt for her. And maybe he was afraid of what she felt for him too, because telling him she loved him hadn't changed things, either. She didn't know why.

He did love and he loved passionately, but he'd spent so many years fighting it there was clearly nothing she could do to change his mind.

Just like when her mother had cut off all contact, Anna hadn't been able to change her mind either.

You're not enough for him. You'll never be enough and you know it.

The thought was so painful that she eventually took herself into the shower, ending up sitting on the floor weeping for a lonely man who couldn't acknowledge his own need for comfort and love. A cold and unyielding mountain.

Eventually, she hauled herself out and dressed, just as someone knocked on her door. Her heart leapt and fluttered like a bird inside her chest, but when she pulled it open it wasn't Adonis, but his brother.

The disappointment was so bitter she could hardly bear it.

She wiped ineffectually at her cheeks, but was too tired to pretend she hadn't been weeping. 'What do you want?' she asked, not bothering with any proper form of address, despite his being a royal prince and she nothing but a banished nun.

Prince Xerxes was tall and ridiculously handsome, his dark eyes glinting with gold as they surveyed her. 'Are you going to invite me in?' he asked eventually, his tone neutral. 'Or are we going to have this conversation in the hallway? I am a prince, you know.'

Anna sighed and gestured for him to enter, since it didn't look as if he was going to go away.

'Why are you here?' she asked, closing the door after him, her voice raw and scratchy.

He gave her a long, considering look, then without a word vanished into the bathroom, coming back a minute later with a box of tissues. 'Here,' he said, handing it to her. 'You look like you need these.'

Not in the mood to argue, Anna took the box and sat down on the edge of the bed, blowing her nose determinedly and wiping her face.

'So,' Xerxes said slowly, 'my brother stormed out of here a little while ago looking like he wanted to chew through a palace wall with his teeth. And, since he told me earlier that apparently you were going to marry him, I thought I'd better come and see what all the fuss was about.' His gaze settled on her, concern in his dark eyes. 'What's happened, Anna?'

Her throat closed at the gentleness in his tone. 'There is no wedding. He just told me he's going to send me away.'

Xerxes frowned, muttering something very rude under his breath. 'I see. Did he say why?'

She could feel her eyes getting sore, more tears beginning to gather. 'He made the mistake of falling in love with me and apparently that's a cardinal sin.'

'Ah,' Xerxes murmured, as if that explained everything. 'I expect he mentioned that emotions are bad.'

'Yes.' Anna wiped away another tear. 'I told him it didn't matter that he couldn't love me back. That I didn't need it. I just wanted to love him, because he needs it so badly...' She stopped, because there was no point going on. 'It doesn't matter now. He won't change his mind; I know that much.'

Xerxes was quiet a long moment. Then he muttered, 'My brother is a fool. He's taken on too many of our father's lessons, that's the issue. And he's so damn stubborn.'

'I know.' She blew her nose again, debating whether to tell him that she was pregnant and then decided not to, since Adonis obviously hadn't mentioned it to him. 'He wants me to leave tomorrow morning.'

Xerxes frowned. 'Do you want to go?'

She thought about it. She thought about insisting on staying, on fighting for the man she loved, crushed beneath the crown he wore. But she'd tried that before and it hadn't worked, so why would it work now? She'd thought her love would be enough to move him, but it wasn't.

Which left her with only one option.

'Yes,' she said thickly. 'I need to go home. Back to the convent.'

The prince's face was expressionless, but something shifted in his dark eyes. 'If you would prefer to leave earlier and not at His Majesty's pleasure, I can arrange that for you.'

Yes, she could go tonight. She didn't have to wait until he got rid of her.

It wasn't much of a power move, but it was better than nothing.

Anna took a deep breath, wiping the remaining tears from her face, and met Xerxes's steady gaze. 'Yes, I think I'd like that.'

He nodded. 'You'd better start packing, then.'

Then she remembered something. 'Xerxes, I need Ione to know that I'm not leaving because of her. That I would have stayed if I could.'

'I'll tell her.'

Tears threatened again, but she fought them down. 'She's a special little girl. Adonis needs her so much.'

'Oh, I know. And don't worry.' There was a fierce glint in Xerxes's gaze all of a sudden. 'I'll make sure he's made aware of that.'

The next morning, Adonis made preparations to fly Anna back home to England, only to discover that she'd already gone. Apparently, she'd left in the depths of the night in one of the royal jets, courtesy of his brother.

He wasn't upset. Any pain he'd felt earlier was gone. He felt nothing, only a sense of… heaviness. As if something weighty had descended on his shoulders, something that would be there for ever.

But that was fine. He was carrying the heavy

burden of his country anyway, so what was a little more weight?

He adjusted his arrangements, sending one of his aides to England instead to keep him up to date with the progress of her pregnancy. A decision needed to be made about that, but he had a few weeks yet; he'd make it closer to the time.

Right now, though, there was a wedding to be cancelled, not to mention other decisions to make, including finding a new companion for Ione.

He was in the middle of working through a stack of papers that afternoon, when the doors of his office flew open and his daughter came racing in, tears staining her face.

He frowned at her, a pang of something echoing inside him that he reflexively ignored. 'What's wrong?' he asked, putting his pen down. 'Where is your—'

'Where's Anna?' Ione demanded. 'I want Anna!'

Another something in his chest shifted, making it tighten. 'She had to go home to England, little one.'

'No!' Ione shouted. 'You told me she was

going to be my *mama*. You said we would be a family.'

A sense of pressure increased in his chest, like someone pressing a hand down directly above his heart. 'That's not going to happen now,' he said firmly. 'She had to—'

'I hate you!' Ione's bright blue eyes, so like his own, were burning with rage. 'I hate you, Papa!' Then she turned and ran out of the room, weeping.

Adonis's jaw tightened, the pressure on his chest intensifying. He ignored it. She would learn, as he had, what it meant to sacrifice everything for the throne.

'Don't become him...if not for my sake, at least for hers.'

Anna's voice wound through his head, but he had no time to dwell on it, because Xerxes was suddenly strolling in, his dark eyes far too sharp for Adonis's liking. 'Ione is not happy with you, apparently,' he said casually.

'Get out,' Adonis ordered. 'I have work to do.'

'Or perhaps a high horse to sit on.' Xerxes ignored him, coming up to his desk. 'Tell me, is it cold up there, Your Majesty? Is it comfortable?

Does it matter that you've broken a woman's heart, not to mention your daughter's?'

Adonis didn't think that relentless pressure inside him could get any worse, but apparently that wasn't the case. It felt as if he was suffocating.

He kept himself very still, because if he moved he *would* suffocate. Either that or he'd explode and Xerxes would get caught in the fallout. 'I don't recall asking for your opinion, Xerxes. What I would like you to do is get out...'

His brother leaned over his desk and casually knocked his stack of papers over, scattering them on the floor. 'Look up and pay attention,' he snapped. 'The best thing to come into your life since Ione has gone and all you can think about is your work? Are you as blind as you are stupid?'

Adonis wasn't sure if it was the papers that broke him or Xerxes's insolent tone. Or that after Anna his detachment was irreparably damaged and nothing could fix it.

Whatever it was, right in that moment, fury rose, thick and hot, and he was out of his seat, coming around the side of his desk. He took his brother by the shoulders and flung him up against the wall before slamming an arm across his throat. 'Don't you *dare* speak to me like that.' He wanted his voice to be cold, but it wasn't. It was hot, gravelly, and full of rage. *'I am the king.'*

Xerxes didn't fight him and didn't move, but gold gleamed in his eyes. 'You're not a king. You're an idiot. You love her.'

'I can't love her,' Adonis ground out. 'Love can be used—'

'Why did you send her away?' Xerxes interrupted, as if his brother's arm wasn't pressing against his throat. 'She loves you, brother. Her tears broke my heart.'

He'd thought that after facing Anna the night before he'd got rid of his emotions. That he would never feel anything again. Yet here he was with fury eating him up inside and guilt following on behind, along with grief and pain, and all those other emotions he'd been struggling his whole life to ignore.

They were cracks in his detachment, in his soul, fracturing him like veins of magma in a volcano, weaknesses undermining the strength of the whole. And they were getting wider, spidering out, making him feel as though he was going to break apart.

'I had to send her away,' he said roughly. 'A king cannot—'

'A king can do whatever the hell he pleases.'

'No.' He forced his arm harder against his brother's throat, his heart beating hard in the cage of his ribs. The cracks widened and he tried to stop them, tried to keep himself together. 'You of all people should know what love does to someone. What it did to me.' He was breathing faster now, the tangled wave of emotion boiling up inside him making those cracks turn into fissures, great chasms that would swallow him whole. 'What it did to you, Xerxes. What our father did to you. And all because of me!'

Strangely, the look in his brother's eyes softened. 'I know, Adonis.'

'I could have saved you.' The failure of it choked him, guilt strangling him. 'If only I'd stood up to him. But I didn't. Because I wanted his approval. I was desperate for it.' He could hardly breathe. 'I put my need ahead of your pain, ahead—'

'Adonis,' Xerxes said quietly. 'Let it go.'

'How can I do that? After what you suffered? After how I failed you?'

'You were just as much a victim as I was.' Xerxes's gaze was very direct, very steady. 'And my suffering led me to Calista. Believe me, brother, I would go through it all again, every second twice over, if it meant I got to have her in my life.'

His jaw was tight, his body ached. 'I can't let it go. It's not that easy.'

'I know it's not,' Xerxes said. 'But if I found the strength to step away from Xenophon's shadow, then so can you.'

'How?' He searched his brother's face. 'I don't understand how it's possible.'

'Look into your heart, Adonis. That's where your answer is. That's where your true strength lies.' A fierce light burned suddenly in Xerxes's eyes. 'That's where I found mine. In my wife and in my daughter. In my love for them.'

Every muscle in his body was tense. He felt as if he was in the middle of a battlefield.

How could love be a strength when it had been nothing but failure and pain for him?

Anna knows how.

Something surged through him, something that felt like rage and yet wasn't.

His little nun. His brave little nun. Who loved without fear and without reservation. Who didn't cut herself off or detach herself. Who threw herself passionately into everything she did, including caring for his daughter.

Including loving him.

She is so strong. How could you think she would fail you?

He went utterly still, frozen rigid where he stood as the thought hit him. She'd told him she loved him and he'd ignored it. Dismissed it. All the important people in his life had failed him, so why wouldn't she?

'That's not strength. That's fear...'

He'd dismissed that too, because he wasn't afraid.

Or was he? Was that the real truth? That deep down he *was* afraid? Afraid of all those emotions burning inside him. Afraid to let himself feel. Afraid to let himself trust. 'How do you know?' he asked in a voice that didn't sound like his. 'How can you ever believe someone when they tell you they love you?'

Xerxes stared at him a moment longer. Then

he shrugged. 'It's called trust, Adonis. You can only trust them.'

'I don't know…' His voice was cracked and broken. 'I don't know if I can ever trust anyone.'

'You can trust her, though,' his brother said quietly. 'Her heart is big enough for both of you.'

And he was right, wasn't he? His little brother was wiser than he was. Because if there was one person in all the world he could trust, it was his indomitable little nun who'd told him she would wait for ever for him.

She won't fail you. You cannot fail her.

He could feel it then, the cracks running through him, but they weren't fissures or chasms after all. They weren't going to swallow him. They were letting the light in, pouring all over him, engulfing him in warmth. In strength. In certainty. A certainty he hadn't felt for years. And this time he didn't fight it, he embraced it.

It didn't matter if one day she might feel differently. It didn't matter if one day she changed her mind or found someone else more important to her than he was.

What mattered was that *she* was important to *him*. She was more important than anything in his entire life, except possibly Ione.

She was certainly more important than his throne.

And this was a choice, his last choice.

So Adonis Nikolaides chose.

'You're right.' He looked at his little brother, his heart thundering in his chest. 'I need her back, Xerxes. I need her back right now.'

'Of course you do.' Xerxes smiled. 'And I have a very good idea how to go about it.'

CHAPTER TWELVE

THE FLIGHT TO England was interminable, the journey back to the convent deep in the rolling green hills of the English countryside even longer.

But Anna didn't care. She found she didn't care about much at all.

It was late and the Reverend Mother received her with little fanfare, apparently not requiring much of an explanation. She showed Anna back to her little room without comment, which was good because Anna didn't want to talk and was pathetically grateful she didn't have to, falling into a restless sleep the moment her head touched the pillow.

The next day she didn't feel any better, gritty-eyed and hollow inside. Some of the other nuns wanted to hear about Axios, but she didn't have the heart for conversation, staying in her room instead, lying on the bed with her arms wrapped around herself, trying not to think of Adonis or Ione.

Trying not to think of what she'd left behind.

She didn't know what time it was when there was a quiet knock on her door and it opened to reveal the Reverend Mother. She looked at Anna for a moment, then said quietly, 'You have a visitor.'

Anna shook her head. 'I'm sorry, Mother. I'm not up for visitors today.'

'Nevertheless, I think you'll want to see this one.' The Reverend Mother's lined face softened. 'He's waiting in the garden and he said he'd wait there all day if he had to.'

Everything inside Anna went still.

No. It couldn't be…

She didn't want to hold on to hope, so she tried not to as she walked the convent's echoing halls and out into the tiny walled garden with the roses climbing up the walls.

Yet hope burst out of her all the same, opening its wings and flying straight into the sky when she saw the tall, powerful figure waiting beside the fountain.

She froze, unable to move, her heart shuddering in her chest.

And then the figure turned and her heart plummeted.

It wasn't Adonis. It was Xerxes.

'What are you doing here?' Anna demanded, agony crawling through her.

Xerxes, against all odds, smiled. 'I'm here on behalf of my brother. He's been unavoidably detained, so he sent me to ask you if you'd like to attend a wedding.'

Anna blinked. 'A wedding? What wedding?'

Xerxes's smile grew even warmer. 'Your wedding.'

Shock moved through her and for a minute she had no idea what to say. 'Mine?' she eventually forced out. 'What do you mean?'

'The king wants to know if it's still true. If you're still waiting.'

She shuddered.

'Yes,' she said hoarsely, before she'd had time to think. 'I am.'

'In that case, he told me to tell you that "never" came sooner than he thought and that you're stronger and braver than he'll ever be. And that he loves you more than he'd ever thought possible.'

Anna felt unsteady, the world upending under her feet. 'I don't…'

'But don't take my word for it,' Xerxes said. 'If you come with me he can tell you himself.'

Everything was the same. Nothing had changed. She still loved a lonely mountain of a man who'd cut her out of his life. Who'd told her that he would never wake up one day and realise that he wanted her love.

But it seemed as if never was here. And she had nothing better to do. The convent was still a prison. And there was a wedding. *Her* wedding.

'Anna,' Xerxes said gently when she didn't move. 'Please. He needs you.'

She didn't know what that meant, and Xerxes wouldn't explain, but in the end she went with him, shocked when she was taken from the convent to a private airfield and the royal jet took off up into the sky.

On the plane, Xerxes showed her a room where a simple, long, white, silky dress was hanging, plus a raft of feminine beauty products, hairbrushes and pins and make-up.

A wedding, Xerxes had said. Her wedding.

Anna's heart thumped hard, and after Xerxes

had closed the door behind her she stared at the dress on the hanger. Her wedding dress.

With shaking hands, she took it off the hanger and put it on. It fitted perfectly.

She paused over the make-up and then settled for her hair loose over her shoulders and a bit of lipstick. She didn't need blusher. Her cheeks were already glowing.

And when she came out of the room, Xerxes's smile filled the entire cabin.

Then there was nothing to do but wait.

Eventually, the jet touched down in Axios and she expected to be taken to the cathedral. Instead she was taken to a helicopter and bundled inside, and then they were flying over the mountains and across the sea, to a small, familiar island.

Anna's eyes filled with tears as the helicopter touched down and the doors were opened, and then Xerxes was guiding her out of the machine and along a rocky path strewn with white rose petals that led to the sea.

And there on the pure white sand, with the blue of the ocean beyond, stood a man.

Just a man.

He was tall and broad and powerful, and he

wore a simple white shirt with black trousers. His feet were bare, and pinned to his breast was a gold crowned lion.

He was looking at her and his eyes weren't cold; they were a fierce bright blue, full of heat, full of the passion that burned in his soul. The mountain had become a volcano.

Anna's throat closed and the tears threatened to spill, but when a little girl with bright red curls dressed in a sparkly white dress rushed up to her and thrust a bouquet of sea lilies into one of her hands while taking the other, Anna held on tight. And together they walked towards the man waiting on the beach.

There were only three others watching, Xerxes and his wife, Calista, and the priest standing with Adonis.

And when Anna arrived at last by his side he held out his hand to her, and the love and fierce possession that shone in his face made her heart tremble in her chest.

'You came,' he said, his deep voice hoarse as he took her hand in his. 'I wasn't sure if you would.'

'I told you I'd wait.' She took no notice of the

tears on her cheeks. 'And I would have waited even longer.'

'I didn't want you to.' He brought her hand to his mouth, kissing the back of it, passion blazing in his eyes. 'You already waited too long for me to come to my senses. Forgive me, little nun. I've caused you such pain.'

Anna's tears fell and she didn't wipe them away. 'There's nothing to forgive. You were just afraid and I understood that.'

'But I never meant to hurt you.' He turned her hand over and kissed her palm, keeping his gaze on hers all the while. 'I should have trusted you and I didn't. All I ever wanted was someone to put me first, to be more important to someone than a throne. But when you gave me that… I couldn't take it. Because you were right, I was afraid. I told myself I was afraid that you would fail me somehow, but it wasn't that. It was the pain I was afraid of.'

Her throat closed in helpless sympathy. 'Oh, Adonis…'

His eyes gleamed hotter, fiercer. 'I thought my detachment would save me from that, but it didn't. There was too much inside me, all those feelings I'd been denying. I couldn't shut them off. Then someone I know pulled me aside and told me what a fool I was.' He glanced over to where Xerxes stood and smiled. 'He told me where to find the strength I needed to step away from my father's lessons. To overcome my fear.' Adonis glanced back at her, the fierce love of the man shining in the king's eyes. 'It was you, little nun. You're my strength. You showed me how to love without fear, how to love with passion and bravery. You would never fail anyone. And so I don't want to fail you. I want you to teach me new lessons, better lessons. I want you to bring happiness into my life and I want so much to bring it into yours too.'

Anna couldn't stop her tears and she could barely speak, her throat was so tight. 'I want that,' she forced out, her voice husky and raw. 'That's all I ever wanted.'

His smile was like the dawn after a long, dark, lonely night. 'Then marry me, Anna. I should have come for you myself, but I wanted this to be a surprise for you. And I wanted to give you a choice too.'

Anna took a shuddering breath. 'My choice will always be you, Adonis.'

His gaze was bluer than the sea behind him.

'I always chose my crown before. But not today, little nun. Today, I choose happiness. Today, I choose you.'

And so they were married on the beach, with no fanfare, only family and a priest.

Not a nun and a king.

Just a man and a woman.

And after the ceremony Adonis took her into his arms and kissed her passionately and for a long time, much to Ione's disgust.

Then much, *much* later, after celebrations with their family and after Xerxes, Calista and the priest had got into the helicopter and gone, Adonis and Anna let their little girl put Anna's bouquet into the sea as an offering for Ione's mother.

'Will she get it?' Ione asked her father as it floated in the waves.

'Yes,' he said quietly. 'She will.'

Then, as Ione scampered down to the water's edge to play, Anna leaned back in her husband's arms, his body tall and powerful against her back, a mountain protecting her, sheltering her. Loving her.

'You haven't said it, you know,' Anna murmured, watching the moonlight on the waves, and listening to Ione's laughter.

'Said what?' Adonis's breath was warm against her neck.

He was teasing her, of course he was. 'Xerxes told me to come with him so I could hear it from you myself.'

'You're mine.' His lips brushed against her skin, making her shiver. 'Is that enough?'

Anna turned in his arms and looked up into his strong face, meeting blue eyes gone dark as midnight. 'And are you mine, Lion of Axios?'

He smiled just for her, lighting up her heart. 'Of course, Anna Nikolaides. Who else's would I be?'

Her new name made her happiness overflow inside her. 'Say it.'

His expression intensified, blazing into hers. 'I love you, little nun. I love you, my wife, my lioness, my strength. I love you, Anna.'

'And I love you, my husband,' she whispered back.

He kissed her under the moonlight, there on the beach, with Ione's laughter in their ears. He was a king and a lion. A mountain and a man.

But most importantly of all, he was her love. He was her heart.

He was her home.

He was hers.

EPILOGUE

XERXES LOOKED INTO the crib and pulled a face. 'Twins? Really, Adonis? You always have to go one better, don't you?'

Adonis, feeling very smug indeed as he looked down at his two sons, laughed. 'What did you expect? I am a king.'

Ione stood on the other side of the crib, looking as smug as he felt. 'Achilles and Hector,' she pronounced. 'Those are their names, Papa. And they're my Defenders of the Throne, aren't they?'

'They are,' Adonis agreed. 'Both of them.'

'God help them,' Xerxes muttered. 'She's been reading too many myths.'

But Adonis wasn't listening. He was already turning back to the bed where his beautiful wife lay, resting on the mound of pillows he'd arranged behind her head.

He sat down and snuggled her into his arms, every muscle in his body relaxing as she turned her radiant smile on him. 'We should keep those names,' she said.

'Really? You like them?'

'Yes.' Her smile deepened. 'They're heroes. Just like their father.'

'Next time, I want heroines,' he said and kissed her. 'Just like their mother.'

Anna gave a long-suffering sigh. 'There won't be a next time. Not after that.'

But there was. And another. And then again.

Because, though the Lion of Axios was a stern and regal king, Adonis Nikolaides was a man who turned out to have an unlimited appetite for laughter and joy and happiness. For his wife.

And for love.

Always love.

* * * * *